I HEAR YOU

PRAISE FOR *I HEAR YOU*

'These moving short stories are brave, honest, raw and funny, doing what fiction does best, showing us the lives of others and in so doing showing us ourselves. Wonderful.' —**Kit de Waal**

'The stories in *I Hear You* are full of tenderness and fun, reality and rawness. In every one, there is humanity and wisdom. As a reader, you are in for a treat because Paul McVeigh is a born storyteller and his imaginative vision is compelling.'
—**Wendy Erskine**

'From a son paring the bunions on his mother's feet to a man's soul getting sealed out of his body, and culminating in a deft interlinked cycle, the stories of *I Hear You* are warm, frank and unsentimental, bursting with character and idiosyncratic detail, written with Paul McVeigh's characteristic geniality and Belfast wit.' —**Lucy Caldwell**

'This is a world of escape artists and fraudsters, of body swaps and comedy cuckoos, of misfits and trespassers of every ilk. We are moved and entertained in equal measure by the antics of the spangled cast of "The Circus", a club that is peopled, in the words of Dockyard Delores, by 'the freaks, the fruits, the rejects, the weirdos'. Where else would you want to be than amongst the outliers, where the tender, the vulnerable and the brave reside? There is no better company to be in.'
—**Bernie McGill**

PRAISE FOR *THE GOOD SON*

'When I think of exceptional working-class novels from the last few years, I inevitably think of Kit de Waal's *My Name Is Leon* and Paul McVeigh's *The Good Son*.' —**Observer**

'Blackly hilarious (with) one of the most endearing and charming characters I've come across in a long time.'
—ELLE Magazine Best of 2015

'The backdrop is one of poverty, paranoia and violence, both sectarian and domestic . . . there's no nostalgia in the depiction of simmering brutality and intense claustrophobia . . . a full-colour close-up of life in a no-go area. Heartbreaking . . . gripping.' —**Guardian**

'Paul McVeigh's debut new novel is everything its fans say it is – funny, raw, sometimes distressing, always wonderfully entertaining. The young Mickey Donnelly is a superb creation, his thoughts and feelings bubbling onto the page in an immaculately-rendered voice, droll, cheeky and authentic. McVeigh renders a child's view of a very adult nightmare with bewitching empathy. You will love every moment of it.' —**Jonathan Coe**, author of *The Rotters' Club* and *What a Carve Up!*

'Pungently funny and shot through with streaks of aching sadness. Scenes from it are going round in my head months later. Paul McVeigh's is an original voice of which I, for one, can't wait to hear more.' —**Patrick Gale**, author of *A Place Called Winter* and *Notes From an Exhibition*

'One of those books that's written in such an accomplished and natural way that it seems not like a book at all, but a perfect, fully-formed rendering of reality through another's eyes. It's a triumph of storytelling, an absolute gem.' —**Donal Ryan**, author of *The Spinning Heart*

PAUL MCVEIGH's stories have been in numerous anthologies including *Being Various*, *The Art of the Glimpse* and *Common People*. They have also appeared in *The London Magazine*, *The Stinging Fly*, *The Irish Times*, on *BBC Radio 3, 4, 5*, and *RTE Radio 1*, as well as, on *Sky ARTS*. His ten-part short story series, *The Circus*, aired on *BBC Radio 4* in 2023 and was repeated on *BBC Radio Ulster* and *BBC Radio Foyle*.

Paul co-edited the *Belfast Stories* anthology, edited *Queer Love* and *The 32: Anthology of Irish Working Class Voices*.

Paul co-founded the *London Short Story Festival* and was an associate director of *Word Factory*, 'the UK's national organisation for excellence in the short story'. *The Guardian*.

Paul's debut novel, *The Good Son*, won *The McCrea Literary Award* and *The Polari First Novel Prize* and was shortlisted for many others including the *Prix du Roman Cezam*. His writing has been translated into eight languages.

ALSO BY PAUL MCVEIGH

The Good Son (2015)

PAUL McVEIGH

I HEAR YOU

SALT
**MODERN
STORIES**

CROMER

PUBLISHED BY SALT PUBLISHING 2025

2 4 6 8 10 9 7 5 3 1

Copyright © Paul McVeigh 2025

Paul McVeigh has asserted his right under the Copyright, Designs and Patents Act 1988 to be identified as the author of this work.

This book is sold subject to the condition that it shall not, by way of trade or otherwise, be lent, resold, hired out, or otherwise circulated without the publisher's prior consent in any form of binding or cover other than that in which it is published and without a similar condition including this condition being imposed on the subsequent publisher.

This book is a work of fiction. Any references to historical events, real people or real places are used fictitiously. Other names, characters, places and events are products of the author's imagination, and any resemblance to actual events or places or persons, living or dead, is entirely coincidental.

First published in Great Britain in 2025 by
Salt Publishing Ltd
12 Norwich Road, Cromer, Norfolk NR27 0AX United Kingdom

www.saltpublishing.com

Salt Publishing Limited Reg. No. 5293401

A CIP catalogue record for this book is available from the British Library

ISBN 978 1 78463 344 8 (Paperback edition)
ISBN 978 1 78463 345 5 (Electronic edition)

Typeset in Granjon by Salt Publishing

Printed and bound in Great Britain by Clays Ltd, Elcograf S.p.A

Dedicated to my brother Alex who heard me.

Contents

Introduction	xi
Tickles	1
Cuckoo	10
Daddy Christmas	18
THE CIRCUS	29
The Singer	31
The Glamorous Assistant	39
The Irish Dancer	46
The Impressionist	53
The Judge	61
The Comedian	69
The Medium	76
The Drag Queen	83
The Gymnast	91
The Organiser	98
Acknowledgements	107

Introduction

THE STORIES IN *I Hear You* are in chronological order. Tickles was the second short story I'd written, and my first for radio. I was commissioned by BBC Radio Ulster producer, Heather Larmour, and it aired on BBC Radio 4. Although this was the only time we worked together, Heather met with me many times and, over many conversations, mid-wived me through writing for radio, teaching me so much about the medium.

'Cuckoo' was my second story for radio, commissioned by BBC Radio Ulster producer, Michael Shannon, who commissioned all the stories printed here, in fact, bar 'Tickles'. It aired on BBC Radio 4.

'Tickles', a story about Mother and Son, then resurfaced, chosen as Radio 4's Mother's Day story and was used, shortly after, by an English vicar as the basis of his Easter sermon.

The third stand-alone story in this collection, 'Daddy Christmas', aired on Christmas Day.

There's a number of things that you have to adapt to when writing for radio, for example, the story slot is fourteen minutes, and that translates to, roughly, 2,000 words on the page. The story slot is 3.45 p.m. in the afternoon and is to be considered in the story theme and language used. As an ex-teacher school run time was also on my mind.

'The Circus' was a challenge, with a number of firsts for me. I was commissioned to write ten linked short stories with an over-arching storyline, and also, in the post-lockdown world, there was a desire for the story and overall tone to be upbeat.

Writing for radio excited me as coming from a theatre and comedy writing background my ear was tuned to dialogue and oral story telling but it wasn't until I met Cathy Galvin and attended the first Work Factory Salon in London, that I fell in love with short stories. One night a month, short story lovers would gather in a tiny bookshop in the back streets of Soho and listen to the best writers in the country reading their work out loud. Cathy's Word Factory forever entwined in my mind the short story form and hearing a story read aloud, so it's perhaps no surprise that my first collection of stories should be those I wrote for radio.

I HEAR YOU

Tickles

Mum thinks I'm Dad. She's holding me and won't let me go. I could be wrong, but the way she took me by the arms and stared into my eyes before she hugged me, there was just so much love. I've only ever seen her look that way at one person. And you have to give it to the man, even in death, even through Mum losing her mind, he's still making her happy.

I've tensed up. I don't want her to notice and hurt her feelings. I wish I could just let it happen and feel it. Take the affection and pretend it's for me. Steal love from a dead man. Or pretend I'm him, for her.

Is she even in that moment any longer? Maybe she's forgotten who it is she's hugging and why? Staying still out of embarrassment, hoping it will come to her. I shuffle round to catch a glimpse of her face in the window of the conservatory. I'll know then. We sway like awkward teenagers at a dance, but Mum won't turn. Feet planted, her hug tightens.

I feel claustrophobic. For years I hugged Mum and felt her freeze. Tolerating my touch but never returning it. And not once did she initiate it. I've only started hugging her again since she's been gone.

Voices approach. I pull away, gently, giving the polite signal, *that was lovely, Mum, but enough now*, but no reaction from her. What is left of her in there? Even the humiliation of public displays has gone.

Two women enter the conservatory and break off their chat to look at us.

'Ach, hello,' one says, as they head towards us.

I smile and nod, rolling my eyes like, *you how it is*.

'How are you?' She stops beside me.

'Fine.' I push away firmer, but Mum squeezes me tighter and now I'm out of view of the women.

'How's your mammy?' one asks. I twist my neck, but all I can see is the side of a head and one huge hooped earring. I imagine a little parrot perched on it, swinging to and fro.

'Great,' I say and give up straining to make eye contact.

'Ach,' I hear, and the two women shuffle into view to nod at me. One nudges the other.

I've no idea who these women are. Could be Belfast banter. Have I met them in here? Or maybe they know Mum from before everything.

'So, you're back then?' The chatty one shows no signs of moving on.

'Yeah, for a few days, then work, you know?' We're all pretending it's completely normal to hold a conversation while crushed in a WWE death grip.

'Ach.' She looks to the other one, who nods and smiles at me. 'How's her feet?'

I search my mind for a link. 'Great.' I smile. I don't know what she means, but I want them to go away.

'Sure, I'll let you go,' she says, without irony.

'Ok, all the best,' I reply, with an awkward wave.

They smile, nod back and head on. Why is it when I talk to people from Belfast, I feel like I'm in a bad Irish play?

I hear them continue their chat in quieter voices until I'm left in silence with the hug.

'OK, Mum, now, come on we go for a walk.' I pull away – no nonsense.

'No,' she says.

Goosebumps tickle me. Her first word in ten years. Since Dad died and she got *sick*. She's coming back. Some of her. She thinks I'm Dad and she's coming back for him. She's holding on for dear life, afraid he'll leave her again. Or maybe that moment's passed too and she's afraid that if she stops hugging and pulls back it won't be his face she sees. How heartbreaking for her that it will be me.

My shoulders have risen to my ears. I'm not enjoying this. I've had enough. Mum rubs my back. Oh God, it's not going to get funny, is it? If she does think I'm Dad she might get frisky.

I breathe out long and slow like I've been taught.

Mum gently strokes my back. I can just feel her fingertips through my thin shirt. Tickling. Inside me there are shifts and turns, I feel them, like a combination lock clicking into place. The nursing-home smell of toilet and school dinners is overpowered by that of dust burning on bars of an electric fire and the fusty smell of old carpet getting warm. I close my eyes and see dark red, floral-patterned wallpaper and a faded-brown, threadbare, Persian-style rug on the floor.

How's Mum's feet? I think.

Ma's just in from work. 'Do your Mammy's feet,' she says, wrestling with her shoes.

I turn on the electric fire with the plastic coal flickering from a spinning fan over a red bulb. The second her shoes are off, Mum collapses on the sofa like the shoes were a stopper and all the air's been let out of her.

I'm in the kitchen filling the washing-up basin with scalding hot water from the kettle, adding those mysterious healing salts from the cupboard under the sink. An old newspaper from the coal hole is placed on the floor between her feet. I fetch the special knife, and the good towel that's still fluffy. I carry the heavy basin, water sloshing up its sides.

'Be careful with that, wee boy,' she says. My eyes widen, my tongue out of my mouth, my teeth clamped down on it. I did this to stop me daydreaming. Pain kept me present. Mum had taught me that many a time with a slap.

'Are you trying to kill me?' Ma shouts as her feet touch the water.

I chuckle, bringing me back to the nursing home. I laugh into Mum's shoulder, and she hugs me tighter. Now I could cry – hearing her voice again in my head. Even when I dream of her she's silent. I'd forgotten how she sounded, like people say they forget the faces of the dead. And now I have it – *her*. Connected from just one word.

'How are your feet, Mum?' I ask. She doesn't respond.

I think about biting my tongue. Do I still do that? No. Through years of yoga and meditation I've learned other ways to stay in the moment, other than hurting myself. But breathing hadn't come to Belfast back then. Like olives and garlic and women driving cars.

I'm happier – settling into this holding. I mean, it's a nice thing to do. For her. If this is what she wants. So what if I'm pretending to be my dead Dad? I've never heard of anyone doing it, but I guess it's not the kind of thing people talk about.

Will she say anything else, not only now – ever? I take my arm from around her shoulder and search for my phone in my pocket. Mum grabs my arm and puts it back around her.

'I'm just getting my phone,' I say. I want to record her. Before I lose her again.

'No!' she shouts. That's me told. I laugh.

She spoke again. I feel like a father hearing his child's first words. No, that's just weird.

'Mammy, how's your feet?'

She doesn't answer. Mum's feet. Wow. They were seriously ugly. They could have been used on warning posters in GP surgeries for smoking, excessive drug use, or some flesh-eating virus caught from exotic travel. Bunions, corns, little toes the size of knuckles and big toes with joints like elbows.

I'm sitting on the carpet in our old house, the one I had to sell to keep Mum here. My legs wrapped around the basin, staring at her. She's bright red, forehead sweating, and those mysterious salts have turned steam into magic vapour. She's under a spell, transported to paradise.

I put my hands in the scalding water and lift a foot out. I test an area of her heel by running a fingernail along it, to see if the hard skin has softened, and skin peels. With the knife I scrape the hard skin, watching it curl like a hot spoon along a tub of ice-cream. I do the thickest areas first, on the heel and the ball of her foot, then the delicate areas at the side. I work until her skin feels smooth and even squeaks.

I hear voices walking past me in the nursing home, but I don't look up. Mum's tickling my back again and I don't want to break it. What if *she* breaks it? Stops holding me?

My lungs fold.

Breathe. She might never hug me again.

Deep, slow, breath, in.

This must be to do with Dad. She would be more *here* if he was still around in some way. A reminder of what she lived for. Maybe I could pretend to be him when I come. What am I saying?

Deep, slow, breath, out. And another.

If he was the reason she ended up here, isn't it possible I could use him to reverse it somehow? Even just a little? I know he's dead but . . .

We had been expecting Dad to die. He had been disappearing from cancer for a few years. Said our goodbyes a few times. The doctor said Mum's early onset of dementia was triggered by depression and grief. He didn't know that Mum lived for Dad. She was devoted to him. Her mind was wired – set to him. Pleasing him was behind everything she did. Her love for him was a like a thick fog that made it hard for her to see anyone else. Mum lost her mind when Dad died, but from the moment she met him,

Tickles

I don't think her mind was ever hers again. And when he died, her brain turned off. Her body abandoned like a toy without its batteries.

I come back from the kitchen with the talc to see Mum half asleep, whilst sitting up, on our sofa.

'Lie back.' I guide her, lifting her feet. I sit, slipping under her legs and resting her feet on my lap. I stroke her legs with my fingers. I kept my nails long for it. Barely touching her, I run my nails along varicose veins like long, purple branches. Tickling her.

'That's enough, you,' she says, impatient with the pleasure, even in half sleep. Happiness was something to be had for a few moments. Not to be indulged in.

Mum's poor feet . . . Two jobs, both standing, while Dad sat down at his. Long-distance driving. *Long-distance skiving,* I called it. I blamed him for her feet, for her working so hard.

'Where's Daddy?' I asked her. What I was really saying was – *he's not here, he never is, you shouldn't be working like this, but see how I love you, more than him, why do you love him anyway when he's never here, even when he's back from work?*

She knew what I meant. I know that now. Because of what she told me next.

'Did I ever tell you how I met your Daddy?' she asks, eyes shut.

She tells me how she left school at fourteen and went to work in a mill. They made her work barefoot because the floors were so wet. She'd work alongside other girls, nodding to their talk but spent every morning watching the clock, waiting for lunchtime. She couldn't miss Dad.

She'd met him at a dance. So handsome, she said, a snazzy dresser, he could dance like the Devil and charm Death into going next door.

They fell in love.

Dad worked in a factory in town back then and on his lunch break he'd run through the streets of Belfast, three miles to her work. Mum would wait until 1.30 then walk to the small window on the factory floor. She wasn't tall enough to see out, but could stand on her toes and reach her hand out to wave. She knew he was there, on the street below and imagined him waving back.

My father would watch her wave, he told her, and wait till her hand disappeared back into the little square on the fourth floor, then run all the way back to work again, through Catholic and Protestant areas alike, risking his very life, just to see her hand.

I didn't believe it. Dad's side, I mean. She was waving to an empty street. He had made a fool out of her.

'How do you know he was there?' I asked. I watched the fine hairs on Mum's legs stand to attention even though I wasn't tickling her. She closed her eyes.

Mum never asked me to do her feet again.

Mum is tickling my back. Around me the residents are being ferried to dinner. I hold her tight. Mum runs her fingertips over my shoulders, mapping continents on my back. I wait for her to stop. For the moment when she says to herself, 'That's enough'. It doesn't come and I dissolve, like those salts she loved so much.

Tickles

Maybe Dad did run all that way, and back, every day, I think. Maybe he stood in the street, waving to a tiny hand out of a fourth-floor window. Maybe Mum isn't thinking I'm Dad and knows it's me here in her arms. Maybe she wants me to know just much she loves me and she's tickling me because I used to tickle her all those years ago. Maybe I just want to believe it. Maybe I choose to.

'Are you staying with your Mum, for her tea?'

I open my eyes to see a smiling nurse.

'Yes,' I say.

'She was pointing at her feet today.' the nurse says, frowning. 'Has she ever had problems with them?'

'Ah,' I say. 'Do you have a basin?'

Cuckoo

AT FIRST, I thought that old devil of a back problem had returned to haunt me. I assumed the position – lay down, knees up, feet flat on the floor. Unlike Martha, I'm not one for the dramatic, but I did text her to come back ASAP. My no-longer-little niece, Alex, was sat beside me, pulling threads from the fringe of the old family rug that Martha and I would pretend was magical and imagine ourselves floating off to cloudy realms in the sky. I don't know why Martha hangs on to these things. It's like she's stuck in the past.

It wasn't entirely Alex's fault, what happened, she was just so excited and insistent that Uncle Ben give her 'a swing' like he used to. It had been a long time since I'd pick her up and throw her around like she was made of air. I had given in, to distract from the awkwardness that had crept between us – grown up through gaps of absence. As we relived happier times, went whooshing around while singing some silly song we'd apparently made-up once – pop! Something went.

On the floor, inch-by-inch, I rolled over onto my side, and rose, with great care, so as not to wake the beast in my back. At standing, a long, thin, sword of pain thrust upwards, under my right shoulder. That was when I first admitted worrying, stood frozen, afraid to move. I waited in this limbo, staring at where I had lain, the shape of me vaguely there on the scrunched-up rug like a shroud.

Alex got bored of me standing there and went to read a book on the sofa. I hoped whatever was going on would right itself by the time Martha returned from shopping, otherwise I'd have to endure the performance, where she'd make it all about her. I was only passing through, really, on my way back to London. She'd managed to lure me by nagging about us having drifted apart and saying that Alex and I were all she had left, now the nightmare ex had scarpered. I could hear loneliness taking over and I didn't want her hitting the bottle again. She can be a bit of a burden.

I snapped to when Martha finally returned. Things must have looked pretty bad as, when our eyes locked, her face drained white as a ghost. She ordered Alex off the sofa, hurried her into a puffy red coat, then led me gently by the arm.

I wondered if this was it. Would I go quickly, like Mum?

As soon as the front door closed, time sped up, so fast that I missed some things completely. I don't remember the journey to the hospital. I do remember a preliminary once-over where I first heard 'collapsed lung'. I remember Martha leaving to drop Alex at a friend's for the night and returned stinking of smoke while I struggled to breathe. I was furious with her for being so insensitive. She was lucky I couldn't speak.

I remember the consultancy room where the doctor told me I needed a pump inserted into my body. I don't remember how it felt when he cut me open, right there in A&E. Just above my shoulder blade. I do remember the nausea. My insides wanted out of me.

I'll never forget the tube. Its hardness. Nor its seemingly endless journey down through my body. It got stuck on the way and had to be shoved past whatever resistance my body was presenting. I shouted in agony and blacked out, the pain too much to bear, and then with another thrust, the pain woke me to howl and retch. I was told later that my reaction was because the A&E doctor hadn't waited long enough for the anaesthetic to kick in.

After the procedure I never felt quite myself again. It all started with that incision. I was convinced some part of me was lost from the puncture he made. But the pain, the trauma, distracted me from what was really going on, you see. I'm sure if it hadn't been for that, I would have noticed something else at the time.

I would have felt you.

After that, I was permanently light-headed. It was like, with some air gone, there was less of me inside and more room for what was left to float around. I felt detached and distant from the world, from myself. Or at least that's what I felt, inside. You wouldn't have known it from the way I was getting on with Martha.

She was spending every spare minute with me. I think I gave her a fright. Maybe it reminded her of our parents; both left us from this very hospital. Grief wasn't the glue I imagined it to be. For us, it was quicksand that swallowed us both whole. Her crazy ideas about alternative therapies drove us apart: crystals and flower remedies and people making themselves sick. To be fair, she didn't talk any of that nonsense with me. Not once. And she couldn't have been more devoted. I think if they'd let her, she would have moved in right beside me. She brought books, chocolate and proper coffee and insisted on bringing home-cooked dinners every day because I had lost so much weight. It got so I didn't look like myself, never mind feel like myself.

Alex came often too. She loved to sit on the edge of the bed, which was against the rules but when I'd go to tell her off, my mouth would close shut instead and my fingers would go up to her ear and give it a little rub. This would make the both of us giggle for a reason I still don't understand. Ridiculous, really.

The first time I got up to walk around, to begin the exercise regime that would re-inflate my lung, Martha was there, helping me stand. I felt this odd moving sensation in my lower ribcage on the right side, heavy, like a large rock had rolled. Martha joked that maybe I was pregnant. Maybe I was, I clapped back. And we shared our first laugh in many years. I was behaving so out of character; I thought it must have been the medication.

The doctor said the odd sensation was an after-effect of the procedure, but as the days went on and there was no abate, he blamed the medication, then bizarrely 'some patients get depressed' after surgery, which spurred Martha to tell him that grief had hit me hard and I hadn't been the old Ben for a long time. The doctor never quite listened to me the same way after.

I was furious with her, but when I went to give her what for, I just didn't have it in me. Deep down, beneath my anger, a voice inside told me she hadn't meant any harm and reminded me how devoted she'd been. I found myself letting go of the bad feeling, it just evaporated, which took me by surprise, frankly. Something like this would usually have caused a massive rift between us, especially in the last few years.

Martha said she liked this new side to me. This more forgiving, and more affectionate me. Like the old me, she said, but . . . better. We laughed – it was becoming a habit. I didn't know where it was coming from myself. And even more surprising, at times, I found my hand reaching across the bed and resting in hers; found my arms outstretched waiting for a farewell embrace.

The good news was that within a few days the pump, along with the exercise regime, had re-inflated the lung. High with relief, I called Martha with the good news.

I knew removing the tube was going to easier than having it forge a way into my body, but I couldn't have imagined what would happen on its way out. That *I* was on my way out.

Once anaesthetised, the doctor pulled the tube out in one shocking wrench. As my insides adjusted, I watched as it slithered in his hand, and I realised that this alien thing, which had been housed inside me, had become part of me. It was as though the doctor had dragged a vital organ out of my body, leaving behind the open exit in my shoulder and the road the tube had dug deep into me.

I had that feeling of being beside myself, like part of me had followed the tube out. There I was, half still inside me watching the doctor, and half outside myself, watching the scene. I was two. Both.

I could see the cut on my shoulder moving like a mouth, breathing. With each of its breaths I felt more present outside until I couldn't feel inside me at all; couldn't see with those eyes.

The doctor was talking to my body, which sat on the edge of the hospital bed where I'd left it, its back to us, shoulders slumped. The doctor laughed. Not at something I'd said, surely, I thought, because I wasn't in there.

If I concentrated, I could hear the doctor. I was fixed, good as new, he said. I could do everything I did before. Live like nothing had happened and go back to work in the next couple of weeks. But he'd be more inclined to discharge me if I agreed to stay with Martha for a while, let her look after me, until I was myself again.

As I passed through air above them, I felt free of pain; I was no longer that wounded body. I wasn't visible to anyone, but when I raised my arm and stared hard at it, I could see an weedy limb, a smoky wisp of a body.

'Now, let's get you sewn up,' I heard the doctor say, approaching my body with a needle.

I remembered thinking, if all of me was outside, what was left in there? I had wondered what I'd lost of me; which part of me had leaked out when I was opened up, but I hadn't once considered that something else had got in.

I watched the doctor sew the wound. With each stitch I felt lighter. I panicked and flew to the cut as the last stitch was sewn. The last remaining connection to my body was broken. I tried to barge in but was stopped by the barrier of my skin. The doctor covered the wound with a dressing.

I swam in the air around my body. I tried to enter through the nostrils but was expelled. I went in through the mouth and was ejected the same way. I was locked out.

I watched it get up and heard it thank the doctor. Martha and Alex came in. I watched it place a hand on Alex's head and rub the tip of her ear while she giggled. I watched Alex throw her arms around its waist. Watched it embrace Martha with a tear in its eye. From the outside I could see so clearly how different I had become. A tear? How could they not know it wasn't me?

It.

You.

I followed, as Martha drove you to hers and helped you inside the house. Before the back door closed, I saw you look back and straight at me. You saw me. This new me. The old me. Floating there. Didn't you? Was it just the once?

You were given Alex's room, while she shared with Martha. Alex comes to cuddle with you in bed and you watch movies together on my laptop. Mine. Movies we used to watch. Getting back what we had. And more. I see her relaxed with you in a way she never was with me. I watch you recovering, getting stronger, no longer wasting away, while the real me is. I'm getting . . . lesser. I can no longer see myself, no matter how hard I look. The effort seems to lessen me further, so I've given up.

Here you are on one knee running your fingers over the rug where I lay that day. Like you lost something there? Can you really not hear me? Or are you ignoring me?

Martha comes in but you are somewhere else. I watch her watching what she thinks is me. She backs out of the room without talking to you, closing the door gently, so as not to alert you to her presence.

I follow her to the kitchen. She opens the lower sash window, lights a cigarette, takes a drag and rests her wrist on the ledge outside – the smoke plumes full of promise and I wait for some genie released from captivity to form, like in the movies we watched together lying on our magic carpet.

I want to say 'get out of this old house'. I want to tell her to stop smoking. I want to tell her to close the window, she'll catch her death.

I fly into her mouth as she inhales and get sucked into her dark lungs but am expelled with force out of her mouth. I fight through the smoke to try again as she takes another drag, but it's useless. I don't have the strength to keep it up. I don't even know what I'm trying to do.

I give up and fly with the smoke out the open window. Up with the smoke I go as it changes shape all around me. I watch Martha until I'm past the window and she is out of sight. I look to the cloudy realms above. Follow the smoke, try to see myself in it. Watch it disappear around me. Like magic.

I wonder, where does it go?

Daddy Christmas

It's dark outside. Winter dark. Cold, too. But, inside, all wrapped up in a thick duvet, you're roastie toastie. There's a little sniffle, hinting something's brewing – but isn't that all part of the season? Nothing says Christmas like a red nose.

Your WhatsApp group 'Gay Family' – tells you 'Party at Santa's Grotto Christmas Night 8 til Late'. It will be the usual mayhem. The last couple of years you've had neither the desire, nor the energy – up with the twins before the dawn's even cracked.

On the bedside table, unwrapped, books from Jo. She knows you well. A new edition of a James Baldwin classic, what a find, and the Maria Carey autobiography you started last night. You laugh at the mix you'd have hidden years ago. It's not the only thing you kept hidden. There are some benefits to getting older – embracing your contradictions is one, accepting yourself, is another.

You try to remember when opening a present on Christmas Eve became a thing – certainly didn't come from your parents. You settle on Jo hearing about an Icelandic tradition where they give books on the Eve and

Daddy Christmas

read together. You think she heard that one on her scholarship year in the States. Every year she tells you a Christmas-themed fact from around the world.

You consider your journal, next to the lamp: leather bound with a long strap that wraps round, giving the illusion of privacy. Not that it matters – it's been a long time since anyone's shared your bedroom and, besides, all you use the journal for is to write your daily gratitudes. A friend gave it to you – told you how a counsellor advised them to write letters to their younger self – it's healing, apparently. You tired, once, but it felt like picking a scab, and you know what Mum said about that: 'causes scars'.

You spend, or *have* spent, every Christmas with Jo and the twins since her divorce. You've become like a new little family. It's the highlight of your year – sleeping over – Baileys and books – waking up to see the boys open their presents. Not this year.

You've barely met this new man. He was new on the scene but then the pandemic came, bringing him so close to Jo and her twins, so quickly. You weren't in their so-called *bubble*. You're still going for Christmas dinner, though.

Outside has brightened a little, so you wiggle out of your cocoon.

'OK, play Mark's Christmas Songs' you call to the black oblong on the corner shelf. The sound of bells jingling, then a deep, shivery voice trembles right into your heart.

Spuds on, roasting in goose fat – you'd par-boiled them last night. Not to over-egg-the-figgy-pudding, but, they are the most important ingredient of a Christmas dinner and you're going to smash them, so to speak. At least you were left with something to do.

A little sing-along and a dance around the kitchen because you love Christmas. The songs and carols. Tinsel and decorations, cards and pressies. Wrapping paper and bows. One year, you did brown paper packages tied up with string and made the twins watch *The Sound of Music*.

You love turkey, gravy, roast potatoes and sprouts. Love crackers with bad jokes, napping with a stuffed belly in front of the telly. You love it all and refuse to have it robbed from your glittery-Christmas-card-writing fingers by Grinches or bah-humbugers.

Mum loved Christmas too. You remember the December you and Jo went searching for, and found, the presents your parents had hidden. On Christmas morning, you showed genuine surprise. Jo, however, gave herself away – it was written all over her face – and she has never understood how you were able to make yourself forget. It's your super-power, she says.

Driving to Jo's, you're running a little late, so you take the short cut past your parent's old house. You usually avoid this route. A door to the past creaks open and stale memories rush to escape. You see mourners crowded on the driveway, you and Jo at the front carrying a coffin, and, only a few weeks later, another, from the front door. There's a price for loving that long. That hard. That exclusively.

You've always struggled with relationships. Some of your London friends would say you were trying to follow the norm – that, being gay, you were free to set your own rules for what a relationship looked like. But you wanted what your parents had. Maybe playing with different rules from those you wanted love from was part of your problem. Being 'too much' was what you were always told when you were growing up, this is what made you 'gay' to people. And then in London, you found your tribe, where you did finally fit in, but, ironically, you were still 'too much' – in the way you loved – you gave too much and asked for too much in return.

What are you supposed to do with all that love?

Opening the door, you hear the kids scream 'Uncle Mark!' from the living room, then feet slap on the parquet hallway. Two boys, identical, apart from one in red football kit, the other in blue. They'd sniffed out your pretend interest in football many moons ago. Intuitive little buggers, kids are.

Many arms warp around your waist, faces burrow into your soft trunk.

'Hello there – my little elves,' you say, pulling on an ear each, while they 'ouch' with laughter.

'Where's our presents?' Shane asks.

'Don't be so cheeky!' Jo comes out of the kitchen drying her hands on a tea cloth, looking tired and over-it already.

'Oh no, I forgot,' you say.

Faces fall, before – 'Only joking!' and they laugh on cue. 'Two sacks with your names on – the boot's open.'

'Shoes!' Jo shouts – sending them to stamp their feet into wellies at the door. Half-on, they crunch over the gravel, pushing each other out of the way.

'Hello, darling,' Jo says, turning a cheek for a kiss. She smells of brandy – cooking or drinking? – you're not quite sure.

'Where's the roasties?' she asks and it's your face that drops before you remember the tray on the passenger seat. Old dogs and new tricks – it will take a few goes at this other new normal.

You sit where you are told, at the breakfast bar.

Ant hands you a flute of bubbles. 'It's not Christmas until there's a champagne salute,' he says.

Is that right? you think.

'To Christmas,' Ant toasts and the three of you clink with the briefest of eye contact.

Jo knows bubbles give you heartburn, but you smile and sip.

Your place at the stove is taken. You didn't even get to put your roasties in the oven to re-heat. You watch the happy couple. Instead of the teamwork you once shared with Jo, she now follows orders. But, you reluctantly have to admit, she appears to love it. Who knew? She looks at you like 'haven't I struck gold?'.

You hear the boys in the living room and realise you'd become so wrapped up with the show that you'd missed the twins opening their presents and you feel a heaviness above your eyes.

'Why don't you take the boys for a kick-about?' Jo asks Ant. They exchange a look.

'Sure.' Ant holds her hips, pulling her in for a slow kiss. It isn't passionate, as such, it's . . . love. Real love. So intimate you have to look away. It causes a shiver of sadness but you are indescribably happy for her. And a little jealous. That's a mix to process.

'Oh, I've got one for you,' she calls over her shoulder

to me as she closes the door behind the footballers. 'My friend, Laura, who lives in Mallorca, told me that in her little town, it never snows, except in the mountains, so at Christmas the farmers bring truckloads of the stuff to the town square for the kids. They play with it until every last bit has melted.'

'I love that,' you say, smiling, while you look at the floor like you are there, thousands of miles away.

'Don't tell Ant,' Jo says as she leans on your shoulder, 'but the boys really missed you last night. Christmas Eve wasn't the same without you.' She smiles. And you do too because she knew it was all you needed to hear and at that moment you couldn't love her any more.

While Jo and Ant wash up, you and the boys watch *Elf*, without the grown-ups, and you like this new alone-time with them. You leave straight after though because you don't like driving in the dark.

As you pull away, they wave from the porch, like a perfect family. And you feel your heart held in a hand that's squeezing too tightly. Those boys had been yours for a while and now they're someone else's.

A reality presents itself. A forgotten life. A trick age plays – you chose a path and the others grow over, until they've disappeared. The lives we choose – and the ones we are given.

You had always wanted a kid.

Yes. All through your twenties. And thirties. Back then it was practically unheard of for a gay man to raise a child. You had always wanted to get married too. Now that you can, you're too old, too set in your ways. Too tired and too selfish, if honest.

You're still thinking about your child when you reach home. Still, when you lie down for what has become your daily nap. You wonder if you'll remember this whole other life when you wake up, or forget again.

You jolt upright, grab your journal, unwrap the long leather tie and take the pen that's clipped onto the cover. You find an empty page and write a letter, not to you as a child, as your friend's therapist had suggested, but to the child you never had.

You write . . .

Dear . . .

I never gave you a name.

To be honest, I always leant towards a boy. I'd have worried if you'd been a girl – scared I couldn't protect you. Look how the world is stacked against girls. Look how your Auntie Jo has to fight. Though I've always felt an affinity with women, a short hand. And, by far, they have accepted me more. But something happens to my body when I say the word 'son', like a tuning fork hitting the perfect note.

As a baby, I'd have smothered you with kisses. I can remember with your cousins – James and Shane – one kiss on the forehead lead to me giving a hundred more.

You'd have been a talker, no doubt – you come from a long line of storytellers. And you'd have loved books. I'd have read to you every night until you drifted off. We'd have listened to books on long journeys in the car too.

Music will take a whole letter on its own.

I wanted to tell you so many things . . . God, where do I start?

Well . . .

Be honest and true.

Make yourself vulnerable and see how people match it.

Take a chance on the world. Risk it all.

And when people lie or hurt you, don't let it close you up or give up trying. Don't end up a lonely old fool like your dad.

Help those who need it.

Be kind.

Give and give and when you think you've given everything, dig deeper, and give what's there too. Watch it all come back to you ten-fold.

Being alive has an impact on the planet – try to cause the least damage you possibly can – to it and the people on it.

Say 'yes' to every opportunity, first. Then learn to say 'no' when needed.

Ask questions and really listen to the answers. Don't go to sleep on an argument. Don't sweat the small stuff. Don't hold grudges. Forgive easy, forgive often, forgive everyone – forgive so much that one day you might be able to forgive yourself.

This is going to sound sentimental, and probably, a little bit daft, but, I really wanted to teach you how to tie your laces. Ridiculous, I know. But I can see it. Me showing you in your trainers by the football pitch. In your new, tight, black school shoes, too. You, frustrated, it would have taken some many tries. Then the day you got there, all on your own, I would have cried. I would have been so proud.

Maybe having you would have solved me. Finally finding something to do with all this love. Are you why I was given so much?

Most likely, I would have been too much for you too – and it would've been the most selfish thing I could have done – having you to fulfil me.

I hope you can forgive me for not giving you life. I hope that you will come to understand in the course of these letters that, in fact, denying myself you was my greatest act of love.

Until next time,
Dad

A beeping phone: Group Chat: 'Don't forget – BYO – And Come to Sleigh and Sashay Away'.

John sends you a private message 'MARK YOU ARE CUMMING lol – No Excuses!'

'Too old', you reply.

'Come on, you can be our Daddy Christmas!' pings back.

You laugh. It's always such a ball on Christmas night – no-one could accuse your Gay Family of not knowing how to party. You place your journal on top of Maria Carey's confessions.

In the taxi, you've a Santa's hat and a T-Shirt that reads *Santa's Little Melter.*

'You getting your head showered from the wife and

kids the night?' says the taxi man to my reflection in his rearview mirror.

You pause – to be or not to be, gay? Coming out is daily event – sometimes multiple times a day – and it's tiring. You decide to save your energy for the night ahead.

'I'm single,' you say. 'But who knows after tonight.'

'Yeoo, big man!' The driver laughs at you and you right back at him.

THE CIRCUS

The Singer

THE FLYER CAME through the door. *North Belfast's Got Talent 2023* at the new club, The Circus. A drag queen on the front. Things are changing round here, that's for sure. Even a few years ago, before I left for college, you wouldn't have got this. I've even heard rumours of a gay night.

There was something about the drag queen. Her face. *His* eyes. But what really got my mind unsettled was the event the flyer was advertising.

Of course, Jane had won it before. Three years in a row; a record. They called it *her* award. They'd joke that no-one else should even bother competing. Then, and I can't remember why, it stopped running for quite a few years. Now, out of nowhere, it was back, bigger than ever, and Jane not here to win it. Someone has to, though, don't they? Someone else has a chance, finally.

My mind found an old shoe box full of memories, and as I opened it, the moths of the past flew out. Years ago – I was nine or ten, maybe – Mammy let us sit up late. Me and our Jane, in nighties, on the floor, leaning back on the sofa. I had my head between Mammy's knees, and Jane's head between

Tony's knees. Our long manes were pulled back, fanned out on their thighs as they brushed in slow, deliberate strokes. It would have been strange with any other male, but it didn't matter with Tony, though we didn't know why, back then.

We should have been in bed, I remember, but when Tony came for visits, all the usual house rules flew out the window. That's why we always loved him. In the street he was very reserved, just like Mammy, but inside, with us, he would become someone else. Like how Mammy became someone else around him. He brought something out in Mammy no-one else did. Something outside of the norm. Without reading too much into it, his difference allowed her to be different.

Mammy laughs when I say things like that. She says I've come back from university like Oprah Winfrey. At first, she was worried I'd get a job using my psychology degree; spending time with 'people like that', I'd become that way too. As if it would somehow rub off on me, or I could catch it like Covid.

Now she's worried about me. It's only taken twenty-five years.

After seeing she wasn't going to convince me to leave psychology behind as a 'wee false start', Mammy, ever the pragmatist, was then determined to help me get some practice, and, hopefully, patients, or clients as she called them. When I told her I was a few years away from having my own practice, she said I could do 'homers', like her hairdresser who comes to our house after he finishes work. Mammy started clearing some things out of Jane's bedroom and putting them in the attic. That blew my mind. That shrine being dismantled was no minor miracle in our house.

Mammy started telling me about neighbours who she knows have problems, like Lily Reid, my old headmistress, who apparently hit the drink something shocking during lockdown, and ended up losing her job.

Mammy's been pointing at people in the street: 'See her, she has that mental health. Riddled with it!' I've given up trying to explain that mental health isn't the name of an illness. There are battles you just have to accept you've lost, in order to win the war. When I made her stop pointing people out, she took to stopping them when I was with her, and asking how they were feeling, and prompting them to share their troubles. Since everyone on the Oldpark Road loves a good moan, they're mostly happy to oblige.

I tried to explain what I thought I'd do with my degree, but the only thing Mammy seemed to have as a reference point was the psychiatrist from *The Sopranos*. She made it clear I'm not to be taking on any paramilitary types, as I could get sucked in by the glamour of it all. And I should stick to women, housewives, who just want to pay someone to listen to them. I could use Jane's room, where my clients could lie down on the bed. According to Mammy, people like to lie down while they're having a moan. She also said she could do their hair and nails while I'm treating them. A family business. She leaves me speechless sometimes. Mammy brought a lovely gay couple down the road over for drinks and I thought, actually, I could help them with their issues, so maybe there's something in this whole 'therapy at home' idea.

Even back then, Tony was bald. He lived alone: no partner, no kids. And even though Mammy had us, looking back, she must have craved adult company. Tony was her only friend. Even though she spoke to some of the women in the street, they were never invited into our house – 'too nosy'. Mammy listened to Tony; she looked at him while he gave advice, with her head cocked to the right, as if to let his words sink into her head through her left ear.

We'd eventually be forced to go to bed, on Tony's visits, despite our pleading and promises of all sorts of great behaviour and help around the house in return for just five more minutes of seeing Mammy the way she was with him. When we'd eventually have our fingers prised from door frames, or if we were particularly stubborn, a stern word from Mammy, we'd sit at the top of the stairs and listen to them talk and roar with laughter. Our Mammy. Laughing. Roaring. Just, wow! We would wonder what Mammy and Tony were talking about that was so funny. We knew, from when we sat up with them – the looks that passed between them over our heads – that there was something secretive going on, naughty even. The childish kind of naughty. It's hilarious to think that there were moments when we even thought something romantic was happening between them. That they were having an affair behind Dad's back while he was away on the rigs.

Years ago, one of those nights with Tony, we were up late, and he said we should all watch this film, told us how fabulous it was. Tony was screaming with laughter

The Singer

at it and seemed to know all the dialogue. He could even do the actresses voices. Tony was so good he should have been an actor himself.

The film was about two sisters. One had been a child star and the other would watch with envy from the sidelines, and I can't quite remember the whole story, except they ended up old and bitter and living together. What I remembered most was that the situation had reversed from their childhood, and the sister who had been sidelined as a child became a movie star when they grew up. The other – the famous cheesy child star with the ringlets and lollipop – her day had passed and she was long forgotten.

I didn't know what Tony found funny about the movie; it was a horror film to me. Tony was in his element and it was at this point, when he was too in his element, that Mammy would usually send us to bed. That's why we would get so mad as things were starting to become fun. He was always hilarious: saying outrageous things about the actors, or TV presenters, or celebrities; whoever was on our screen at the time. That night, he started calling himself Delores, and we were all giggling, including Mammy.

The name on the flyer that came through the door. Dockyard Delores. The eyes confirmed it. And then, a rush through me: the film, and what Tony had said to me.

I guess that night Mammy was more tiddly than usual, because she gave in and let us stay up. Probably because Tony joined in with us too – I think he was loving his adoring audience. Suddenly, Jane threw up all over her nightie. Tony joked that she must have been sneaking some of their alcohol, and the funny thing was, Jane had gone into the kitchen more than once.

Mammy took Jane upstairs to the bathroom and Tony and I were left alone. I'd never been on my own with him and felt this nervous excitement of having him all to myself but I really wasn't prepared for what happened. He told me that he saw me. The real me. That I was like him, but I was too young and wasn't ready to become my true self. He saw how I'd watch Jane while she was performing on stage. He said he didn't need to hear me sing; he knew I was the more talented one. That I was like a superhero who hadn't been formed yet, and was still only the alter ego, like Diana Prince, and one day I was going to realise I was Wonder Woman. For now, I'd have to wait.

I didn't pay much attention to his drunken ramblings, but, remembering it, I was angry. Jane was talented, but so was I. Why was she encouraged and not me? What was the difference? Because she was tall while I was tiny. She was thin while I was dumpy. She was pretty while I was plain. Talent isn't supposed to come in packages like mine. It's not expected, so even if the talent gets recognised, it's a novelty. Even at uni, when I turned away from Mammy and Jane's gaze, I saw that all eyes are the same. Term after term in the drama society, I was offered the roles that girls like me get – the nurse in *Romeo and Juliet*, a witch in *Macbeth*, an old maid; at best, the funny overweight friend.

It's the same with singing; they want Ariana Grande – the full package. People say, sure look at Rebel Wilson, look at Adele: *they* made it. But isn't it funny, those who start big and are proud of it, then lose it all, like it's what they really wanted in the end, deep down. To be thin. Fitting into the dress, fitting into the ideal. Fitting in.

Everyone who met Jane seemed to get out of her way, or paved the way for her. Like everyone was in on a conspiracy to raise her up and hold me down. Jane went from the lead in the school play to lead in youth theatre productions, to small parts in big professional productions, to leads in those too. All the while, Mammy was there, pushing and shoving and showering with her praise. And me, knowing I just couldn't compete with her, I stopped. Now Jane's in London following her dreams. Sounds like a posh Londoner; not a trace of Belfast left. And us, discarded like her accent. Airbrushed out of her life like imperfections in her photos. Calls only when she needs money, or someone to listen to her cry when she hasn't got the part she wanted.

I'd hidden memories, hidden my dreams from myself. Classic. Physician heal thyself, as my old lecturer at uni used to say to us. Maybe I studied psychology to help myself not others as I'd always thought. Now, since I've come home from college, Mammy has transferred all her attention onto me. Even so, when I told her that I'd realised I didn't want to be a psychologist, and about my dream to sing, I didn't know how she'd react. I was ready for her to have a breakdown. I couldn't believe it when she entered me into the talent show. She says I'm to ditch all my clients and focus on my singing career 24-7. And she's moving the last of Jane's stuff to the attic so I can move into the big bedroom. Jane's room.

I feel like a kid again; Mammy making all my decisions for me, but this time I get to be the favourite. To be honest,

I'm enjoying it. Being the most loved. Pushed and shoved and showered with attention and praise.

I will definitely put right all of this and assert my independence, but I'm having a holiday from myself. Letting go of all that pressure of studying, and work placement, and listening to other people's frustrations, hour after hour, day after day. Some *me* time.

Finally, a shot at my dream and this time it will be me feeling the warmth of Mammy's spotlight.

The Glamorous Assistant

He is obsessed. Performing the same old illusions 24-7. I told him, 'It's not healthy, Frank.'

That's how he gets with things, like a dog with a bone. He won't stop till it's been gnawed away to scraps on the floor. But sure, I might as well have been talking to our toaster as him. Maybe I should; I'd get as much back. Frank used to play on that with me; that if he left me, I'd end up like poor Mrs Reid, alone and shouting at an empty house.

I see it all so different now. My eyes have been opened and there's no closing them again. And he's not good enough a magician to put the genie back in the bottle.

When I confront Frank about not answering when I talk to him, he says that he can't hear me when he's 'in the zone'. He's transported somewhere else, especially while he's working on his magic acts in his head. He's so far away, he says, that my voice can't reach him. He asked me if I'd ever heard of the Magic Circle, and I had, vaguely. I thought it was a secret society, like the credit union. Well, here's him to me, that's where he goes – into the Magic Circle – and there's no signal there, like with a mobile phone. I used to believe it too. Now, I think he's been ignoring me this whole time. Makes my blood turn black.

I literally have to go back over the years I've been with him and re-think all the things he told me. I was hoodwinked like his audience. I feel like such a fool. Well, fool no more. And he who laughs last, let me tell you.

I've very mixed feelings about this talent show. I mean, it's been the bane of my life for weeks, with him practicing non-stop, and me forced to watch for hours on end. But, on the other hand, without the talent contest, I wouldn't know what I know now. Maybe, if he'd just stuck to doing his tricks on his own, we wouldn't be here now, but he just had to push it. Push, push, push. Now he'll be lucky if it's not me doing the pushing – him in front of a bus! Not sure if I'd prefer a double-decker or a Glider. Double the height, for the sheer weight of it going over him, or double the length so I can enjoy watching it for longer?

He just had to have the brilliant idea that I would be his glamorous assistant. I told him I didn't want to do it. And, I realise, as the article said, I have to take ownership too; I played a part in our relationship. I have to own it so that I don't repeat the pattern with someone else. And they are so right. I mean, when I look back now, I just went from one manipulative arsehole, God forgive me, to another.

I should have spoken up. Wait, I *did* say no. I've been so confused. That's the goal of gaslighting. The article told me all about it. It's all to make you think *you* are going nuts. Making you doubt your own self rather than doubt *them*.

I said no, but I went along with what he wanted anyway. That's where I went wrong. I should have stood my ground, used my voice. It was because I hadn't found my voice that

The Glamorous Assistant 41

he could ignore me. I've found it now, believe you me. I'm still not using it, but I'm staying quiet through choice. Oh, his day is coming, never fear, and don't you worry, may God strike me stone-cold, paralysed dead. I am done. Over and out!

He knew I was shy, that's what gets me. That's how I know what kind of person Frank really is. Even if I could still believe he just couldn't hear me sometimes – in his Magic Circle – none of that matters because he knows me. Especially after all these years. He knows I hate people looking at me. It's bad enough when you walk into a room and everyone stares; it makes me itchy. It feels like the eyes are literally on me, rolling on my skin. Sometimes I come out in a blotchy rash on my chest. I hate it. And Frank knows that, and he still made me agree to get on stage with him. Roping me in. Actually, roping me in. For his greatest illusion yet. The Disappearing Act. Me tied up in knots, and then 'alakazoo' or 'shish kebab', or whatever. I'm *Gone Girl*.

That film was also an inspiration for my plan. And maybe if he'd watched it with me, like I asked, he would have some warning; but, no, he doesn't watch films about women. You see, like Malcolm said on Facebook Live, once you've made that decision, the universe will make the connections, and you'll see evidence everywhere that you are on the right track.

Now, Frank did say we'd share the prize money, I'll give him that. And here, half of £10,000 is not to be sneezed at. But would he really have given it to me? Or would he have gaslighted me again?

I'm sure that's why I'm grinding my teeth in my sleep.

Stress, the doctor told me. I blame Frank. Just another thing to add to the list. Another thing forcing me out the door. And the more I think of it all, the angrier I am.

You see, it's the way the world works. He causes me stress, I grind my teeth, I go to the dentist, I pick up a magazine, and there's the article all about Frank; not by name, now, but by nature. Him to a T. A gaslighting narcissist. So, he's history, all because he made me be his glamorous assistant, which caused me to grind my teeth, which caused me to discover who he really is. And that's karma biting the arse clean off him. The gaslighting narcissist! I call Frank that all the time, in my head, when I'm with him. Like a chant. Like Tina Turner did in that film to help her leave Ike.

'Don't you remember you were going to . . . ?' he'd say. 'You absolutely said you wanted . . .' and I'd be like, 'Did I? Are you sure?' And if I didn't give in, if I didn't say he was right, he'd explode, or sulk for days. I gave in faster and faster as I knew he'd win in the end so what was the point? It got that I agreed so many times I actually started to believe it.

He had me paying for everything too, I can't believe what a fool I've been. Well, let him try gaslighting when there's no gas! When he finds out I've cut everything off – all the utilities, all his loans I'm paying off every month, everything. I wish I could be there to see his face, but I'll be long gone with the wind.

See, just like Malcolm says, he's been the author of his own exit. And Frank won't see it coming; won't see *me* at all. Ever again.

◊

After all these years. I couldn't believe it when we went to check out The Circus. Frank wanted to see the venue; the stage etc, so that everything would work for his act. We hadn't been since they changed the name, and it'd been renovated and all. And there was James, though I didn't recognise him right away. He'd put on a bit of weight and really filled out, like muscley.

I saw James talking to Tony and I'll admit at first I thought, to myself, like, 'who's that hunk?' James, I mean. I thought maybe it was Tony's new fella, but Tony keeps that whole side of his life private, which I understand; I would too. I mean, I think it's brilliant there's Pride and all, that they have their wee day, but the carry-on of them down that Union Street. Drag queens squealing on them big microphone things – it's a bit much. But they do make me laugh. They just don't give a shite what people think. And you know what, I'm wrong. Why should they care? I'm going to be doing the same from now on, believe you me.

Frank made his way over to James and Tony, and it was when James smiled that I recognised him. I went pure red, just like when I would see him back in school. Luckily, I was behind Frank or he would have clocked it and I wouldn't have heard the end of it, and then the punishments would have started. Frank never lifted his hand to me; there are many ways to hurt someone.

When James sent Frank off with the bar manager to see the stage and all, that's when Tony says, 'Do you not remember James?' And it was like no time had passed, talking over each other and laughing our heads off at our antics in school. Imagine James being rich, and he was the one everyone's been talking about buying the club. We said we'd meet for a drink, catch up on old times, properly. I tried to shush them when Frank was walking back over, but it was too late; Frank heard. Well, I couldn't believe it when Frank was all for it. In fact, he was the one who made us set a date, right there and then, or it mightn't even have happened – we were all just being polite, really.

'Hoist with his own petard!' Tony said, when we met upstairs in the back office of The Circus the next night. It's Shakespeare. I wrote it down when I got home. Tony always was the smart one. It keeps coming true. Frank can't help himself, writing his way out of my life. Frank made us meet because he thought it would mean we had a better chance of winning. 'Get you in with them,' he said to me. 'Give them a sob story and see if they'll fix the contest.' Well, I did give them a sob story; I couldn't stop bloody sobbing. It all came out of me, but it wasn't the sob story Frank wanted it to be; it was everything I'd been holding in for years. I told them about Frank's plan.

I thought I was on my own, that I'd nobody. Frank had made it that way. My friends and then my family. I can see it all now. James and Tony told me to leave Frank. They said they'd help me and we made a plan. It was me who thought of disappearing at the talent show. I'm proud of that. Tony told me about his alter ego, Dockyard Delores. I couldn't believe it. I'd actually seen Dockyard Delores a few times and never in a million years did I know it was him. When he told me, I near died.

◊

In the dead of night when I wake up, my jaw sore from grinding my teeth, I worry. What happens if Frank finds out before or during the escape? What'll he do? And I wonder if it's a bit cruel, humiliating him like that. Maybe it is. But it's just too perfect not to do it. But, also, it's the only time I'll be allowed out of his sight. When he closes that door on his magic box, I'll slip behind the fake panel. Frank will show them all how I've disappeared into his Magic Circle. But when he tries to conjure me back, I'll already be gone. Out the door at the back of the stage and into James's car, and off to the ferry I go, across the water to my new life in Scotland. Tony's sister will be there waiting for me; she's going to help me get settled.

Can you imagine Frank's face? I can't stop laughing. Dockyard Delores is going to pretend like she thinks I've been lost in the ether. Frank might even believe it. Anyway, she's going to distract him as long as she can. How long will it take Frank to find out what's really happened?

I thought no-one round here would remember me if I ever left. Quiet, forgettable me. Now they will. I'll be a local legend. The invisible woman who disappeared.

The Irish Dancer

On my first day at Miss Sanderson's Dance School, I was this scared wee thing. Funny now, to think about it. How I've grown.

I was like that in general back then, to be honest, but that first day, it was like my stomach had frozen solid and it felt so heavy I don't know how I was able to lift my feet off the ground.

Dad used to drive me to Irish dancing before he left and took the car with him. They're really my only memories of him. I think I erased the rest. Who needs people who let you down? I thought it was just men who did that. After seeing the article today, that theory is out the window.

I still think who needs them? Who needs men anyway? Look at Greta Thunberg. Look at my own mum. Look at me. Look at Miss Saunderson. Miss Saunderson: could she really be part of that scandal? I just can't picture her and picture the things they said. It doesn't match.

M'Mummy never learned how to drive. She says that's because in her day, women didn't drive cars, and sure wasn't there buses and taxis. When she says that, m'Granny calls her Zsa Zsa Gabor, which always makes me laugh. Even before I knew who yer women was, I'd laugh, just because the name was hilarious all on its own. I think Zsa Zsa had about ten husbands and was really rich; so m'Ma wasn't really like Zsa Zsa, because she's never even been on a date since Da left, and she's definitely not rich.

I searched online for Zsa Zsa Gabor once. She was a geg. I think she lived in America but was from somewhere in Eastern Europe, and she had this brilliant accent. I watched a clip of her on a chat show in England with this interviewer who had a beard like Wolverine's, in a suit with huge lapels, and she was dressed like she'd just stepped out of her carriage on the way to the palace ball. Thank God I wasn't born back then or I wouldn't fancy anybody. The women or the men. Then again, if I'm really honest, I've never really fancied anyone, ever. I don't think I was born with that thing inside me that makes it happen.

I've always had a crush on Miss Sanderson though. Not like a kissy-kissy crush; I mean, she was – *is* – old, like thirty-something, or even forty or whatever. From the first day at class, the way she carried herself; I'd never seen anyone walk like her before. Maybe some of the teachers at school; but still, Miss Sanderson was in a league of her own. I didn't fancy her; it was more like I wanted to be inside of her body. I wanted to be her. Not now though.

They say, it's completely normal for girls to get a crush on a teacher, and it doesn't matter if they're a man or a woman, it's all part of growing up. I'm just really glad I'm normal in some way; that I actually have had feelings resembling wanting another human being in some actual way that could be mistaken for romantic. And I'm grateful, at the same time, that there's nothing disgustingly physical about it.

I'm never going to have a boyfriend, or husband, or girlfriend, or wife – or kids, for that matter. Everybody stay over there and I'll stay right here, thank you very much. 'Entering My Space is by Invitation Only – No Space Invaders!' I used to have that on a sticker on my school rucksack, next to another with a wee green alien who had enormous almond-shaped eyes. I've got this fantastic new holdall now. Pink. I've written all over it in marker. Save Our Planet. Greta is Our Leader. Wake Up Before It's Too Late.

I tried to talk to Miss about Greta, but she didn't seem to get it. She smiled and looked down like she was bored. Older people just don't understand. Maybe it's guilt as its all their fault we're in this mess anyway.

Miss Sanderson says I'm a natural. Every time a new kid comes to class, Miss Sanderson tells them my story. When she begins, we sit on the chairs that line the back wall, or flop onto the wooden floor we practise on. Miss gets all puffed up with her chest out, sitting with her back straight, and her legs crossed, both hands on her top knee. Crossing her legs makes her skirt rise a little up her leg.

She tells how I came to her class out of nowhere; she'd never laid eyes on me before. Shy and unassuming, not that anyone would know now – and the class laughs. She tells how after three classes, I had to leave the beginners' group because I knew all the steps, and after four classes more, I had to leave the intermediate group because I knew all *their* steps, and before long I knew all the full dances of the advance group, until I had to have a group of my own with just me in it. She tells how, faster than any dancer she'd ever taught, faster than she'd ever known, ever heard of – I was at competitions and slaying all in my path.

Most dancers leave by my age. Miss Sanderson says once girls reach a certain age, they go boy-crazy and start wanting discos, and we all laugh at 'discos', but she winks at me because she knows that they're not called discos anymore, it's just her wee joke, which from anyone else would be cringe, but everything Miss Sanderson does is so cool. She tells them all I can go as far as I want, achieve whatever I want, and not just with dancing. I used to be really scundered with all of them looking at me like I was the Arianna Grande of Irish dancing, but now I don't get embarrassed; I sit up in my chair like Miss Sanderson does, the way real dancers do.

After Dad left, I stopped coming to class because there was no-one to drive me. I was going to walk, but m'Mummy didn't want me going through Ardoyne up to the church hall. Even though we were Catholics too, she said it was too rough there. Then, one day, Miss Sanderson arrived at our front door. She told m'Mummy that I had too much of a talent to let it go to waste, that it would be a loss to the world, that dancers like me come around once in a generation, that m'Mummy had a duty to send me to class, not just for my own benefit but for the history of dance and for Ireland. Well, by the time Miss Sanderson had finished, m'Mummy practically saluted and marched me to the waiting car.

It was on our drives to and from class where I really got to know Miss Sanderson. I asked her about being called Miss; Irish dance teachers always go by Miss, even if they are married and have kids. OK, not the male teachers, obviously, but I've never seen a male teacher, and there's only three boys in our class. Miss said that it was just the way it was, she'd never thought about why the Miss, and she smiled and said it was good that I asked questions and that I shouldn't stop. And I haven't. I've asked them ever since. Of everyone about everything. OK, I've stopped asking m'Mummy because she said it was driving her insane, and she started throwing her slippers at me when it got too much. I've stopped asking teachers at school too because they said I've become disruptive, and the rest of the class roll their eyes and groan when my hand goes up. Mostly, I just ask the internet now. It doesn't mind how much I ask it. In fact, I think it likes it. I ask my phone too, which is sort of the same thing as asking the internet except it can talk back to me.

M'Mummy wants me to enter into this stupid North Belfast's Got Talent competition. I've tried explaining to her that Irish dancing isn't like that. She says sure, our dance school goes to competitions all the time, but a Feis isn't like a talent show. We do dance against each other to see who is the best dancer, but we don't compete against a singer or a man doing the voice of a puppet. I told m'Mummy: 'Miss Saunderson said we are artists.' M'Mummy says I can be an artist every other day for the rest of my life, but for £10,000 I'm someone who enters a talent show. She reminded me of the money she has spent on all the dancing pumps and hard shoes and Feis fees. And especially the dresses; they're so expensive. And she hand-sews all those sequins on. She even takes in work from the drag queen up the street. Her hands are ruined. I felt bad, so I had to say yes. I kept it a secret from Miss Sanderson, but now reading about all the bribing of the Irish Dancing competitions, well, she probably won't even care.

I've only danced locally once before. Our dance school was asked to give a display in Ardoyne GAA. Miss handpicked all the best dancers, and we practiced for it after class when the rest had been picked up by their parents. There were some group dances, but I was asked to do a solo at the end, to close the show. Things were going well until my dance. There was a group of lads laughing in the corner, and the louder they got the smaller I felt. Like I was shrinking. Usually, when I'm dancing, I forget myself; I get into the dance and the music. Everything outside of me disappears. I'm not even sure I'm still there. This time, the laughing kept pulling me back into the room. It was getting between me and the music. I started to overthink about which step was coming next.

I always feel big when I'm dancing, big as the room. I am the whole room. But that night, their laughing got through to me, wherever it is I go. It shrunk me. I became small. A small, scared thing.

It was the only time I ever made a mistake, but I didn't stop; I knew to cover it up. And nobody realised. Nobody except Miss Sanderson. When I finished, and the audience were cheering, I saw her pushing through the men carrying triangles of pints. I know this can't be true, but it was like she was knocking them out of the way, the chairs and tables too, everything in her path flying through the air like she was some sort of She-Hulk. At first, I worried she was raging at me for getting things wrong, even though I knew she wouldn't; but then I saw her turn to the corner where the rowdy group were sitting. Their faces as she approached: laughs turning to frowns, then mouths dropping. I don't know what she said, but it made their faces turn red then purple. A committee man who'd shown us our dressing room came and put their hand on her shoulder, almost like petting a child who was upset. Miss stood solid and still, pointing to the exit, like the statue of a goddess. Two seconds later, the whole bunch of them were thrown out.

Miss used to be my hero. Now, I think Greta is my number one. I mean, Irish dancing isn't important anyway, not like saving the planet is. I promised Miss I wouldn't be one of those kids who'd go boy-crazy and leave dancing. I'm not boy-crazy. I'm leaving dancing because its corrupt and I've found something far more important.

I'm going to dance one last time for Mammy.

At first I thought that if I won the money I could use it to set up my own Irish Dancing School. I'd call myself Miss McClusky. I'd inspire the kids like Miss Saunderson inspired me. But now I know I can't trust her or Irish Dancing anymore. If I win, I'll send the money to Greta, or most of it anyway. I'd have to give m'Mummy some.

If I win, I'm going to give a speech about how corrupt the world is and we have to save the planet. I've got to get them to listen. But first I've got to get on that stage.

The Impressionist

'C OR BLIMEY GUVNOR, an' all 'at. Apples and pears. Yes, we have no bananas.'

Jeff doesn't even look up.

'Chim-chiminey, Mary Poppins.' I do my cockney walk: elbows out, knees out, waddling like a big, fat duck.

Not even the pretend smile he's been doin' lately and here's me makin' a right eejit out of myself. I wish I could leave it be when he's not in the mood, but I can't help it. I tell myself, 'Just stop it, shut up!' But, nah, I hear myself do it again and again. What is wrong with me?

I keep up the cockney geezer, proving I've no control over myself. ''Ere, Mister, 'ow's about I snog the face off ya?'

'Give my head peace, would ye?' says he to me.

I do, because of the tone of his voice. He used to join in with the craic, even if he was rubbish at the voices; he'd give it a go, for the sheer geg of it.

'I've been thinking,' says Jeff, 'this constant joking and putting on funny accents; we're going to make a pact. You're going to get a wee act together, and enter that North Belfast's Got Talent competition so you have an outlet for your amateur dramatics, and then you'll stop getting on my nerves when you're in the house . . .'

'Ach love . . . ,' I start.

'. . . because if you don't, I will do time for murdering you, so help me, God.'

He needs a break from me. I'll get out of his hair.

'OK, then, I'm away on here,' I say. 'Down the shops a minute.'

Jeff tuts and rolls his eyes. He does that when he thinks I'm not listening to him. I am listening, I just don't know what to say. I close the front door, remembering not to slam it, because, recently, it drives him insane. Everything seems to drive him insane at the minute. Everything I do.

I head down the path and along the Oldpark Road to Cliftonville Circus.

'Hello there, Mrs Reid,' says me to Mrs Reid, who's coming out of the off-licence. At this time of day, too. She barely used to drink before lockdown. She's not looking great either; wearing an old coat, and bent over, it's like she's aged ten years in two. It's so sad to see.

'How *you* doin'?' I say in my best Joey from *Friends* voice. She laughs at me. Not sure she got who it was I was doing, but as long as it puts a smile on her face, does it matter? A wee lift to her day. That's what I like to be to people.

I cross Alliance Avenue, even though it's the wrong side of the road to the shops. I'm taking a circle around the Circus. I've always wondered why they don't just call it Cliftonville Circle – what's a circus got to do with it?

Maybe if I imagine someone standing in the middle like a ringmaster. And, while we're at it, I know when people say 'going round in circles' it's a bad thing, as it means not making headway, but personally, I find something relaxing about the shape of it.

I love walking in a circle. The familiarity and routine of it, not going anywhere else, seeing the same faces and the same places. I love having a quick wee geg with the ones who go in and out of the circle most days. And you don't get that moving forward all the time, do you? You don't get to be seeing the same people if you keep going straight ahead; they might walk beside you for a while, but then they'll march ahead or fall behind, never to be seen again.

'Alright, sir! Sergeant Major, sir!' I shout, standing tall, and salute Big Tommy coming from the doctors. I could ask him what's wrong, but not everyone wants you to know their business. Some of us like to keep private *private*.

'Carry on, soldier,' says he and laughs. I wait until he passes and then continue, whistling my way to the funeral home, where I always cross, so I do, and circle back down, past the florist and the solicitors on the corner. I think about a wee extended walk down a bit of the Cliftonville Road, past Little Mo's and the sandwich shop, but my gut says keep the circle tight today. I cross and pass the chippy, and the butchers, and bookies. I run across and pass the newer barbers. Past Boots, and at the zebra crossing there's two kids, so I decide to cross with them for the craic, even though I'll be back where I started a bit sooner than I wanted. I usually like to take it all the way to the Co-op before crossing at the lights.

The taller of the boys is showing the smaller one somethin' on his phone. Looks a bit spicy.

'What's that?' I grab at the phone, but he's too fly and has it inside his school blazer in two seconds.

'Speedy Gonzalez,' says me.

The pups look at me like I'm an oddball. They probably think I'm from Mexico and *speakin' da lingo* myself.

'Pervert,' one of them says.

'It's a cartoon character,' I say. 'YouTube him.' I laugh and rub their heads while they shirk me off.

'Stop touching us; I'll call Childline,' the cheeky one says. These kids are hilarious. They walk ahead of me across the road.

Kids love me, the wee messers. They get me more than adults do. And, here, I tell you what, I can't wait to have my own. If me and Jeff don't start the 'intimacy schedule' soon, those visits with that wee girl up the road who does the counselling will have been a waste of time, and a wee one of our own will get further and further away from us. In her back bedroom, she told us our love life is like a car that's stalled, and we are like two people pushing it to get the engine started again. I don't push it with Jeff, or push the car. And Jeff doesn't push it either. If one of us doesn't start pushing soon, I think our car could end up on the scrap heap.

I have my doubts about someone who works out of a bedroom. I said to our Julie about it, and she said, 'You're gay; why do you need to have intimacy? Sure, it'll be me getting pregnant for yous.' I had to really think about it, but still couldn't find an answer, so I asked Jeff. He said

The Impressionist

it was because if we can't fix the intimacy, then we won't stay together, so 'no us, no baby'.

'Alright, how's himself?' says me to Dave, who's sitting behind the counter listenin' to someone rantin' on the radio. His shop is just off Cliftonville Circus as you head down Westland Road.

'Close the door there, mate,' says Dave. 'Have you not heard of the energy crisis? Do you think I'm made of money?'

I laugh and turn back and close it.

'Keep your 'air on, me ol' cocker,' I say.

I don't know how Dave sticks it, to be honest – that constant rabbitin' on they do on the radio. I said that to Jeff in the car on the way to our big shop at Lidl, and he gave me the funniest look. I don't want us to end up like our neighbours who have nothin' to say each other. I know that because our walls are so thin it's like they're in another room in our house.

'Can't remember what I came in for,' says me to Dave.

'Happens all the time,' says he to me.

He coughs like the aul men used to when I was a kid. The ones that smoked sixty fags a day. The kind that had no tips, and cut the throat of you. I grab some Thai chilli crisps, which cut the throat of me, but Jeff loves. Maybe he'll be up for a Netflix and chilli crisps later on. Bringing date night back might be the trick to start the intimacy off. A wee movie, and his favourite treats, and a wee snuggle on the sofa, and who knows where it might lead. Romance him. Like when we first met.

On the wee noticeboard at the back of the shop, above

the freezer, there's an A4 sheet with two photos. One photo is of a second-hand buggy, and the other is of one of those wee things a baby sits in and it lets them fly about the room even though they can't walk. I don't know what it's called. A walker, maybe? Beside the walker, it says £30 and a phone number. The photo actually has their kid in the walker, which is a bit weird, if you ask me. It looks like the kid has no hair at first, but when you look longer and go closer, it does have. Fine blonde hair. Maybe because I'm so close to the picture my brain is playing tricks on me, because I think I can smell the baby's head. It's milky. Hot milky perfect. I inhale deeply.

'What the hell are you doin'?' shouts Dave to me, and I laugh my head off. He joins in.

'I honestly don't know!' I say. I'm now in absolute wrinkles. 'You'll be havin' me sectioned.'

'Sniffin' pictures would get you put behind bars, never mind,' says he.

'Oh, Jesus, don't be saying that,' says me. He's in kinks.

It's when I come round from my laughing high that I see a poster. It stands out cuz it must've cost a small bomb to get them printed in that thick, glossy paper. Must have money to burn. North Belfast's Got Talent – what Jeff was on about. They do have money to burn. Ten friggin' thousand of the English pounds!

Pictures flash in front of me. That was where I met Jeff. The last time the Talent Show on . . . when was that? Must be four years, nigh. I stared at him the whole night like a weirdo. I know, cuz when I asked him why he waited until the end of the night to smile back, he said he couldn't decide if the staring was cute or scary. But he asked around, and everybody said I was harmless. Or gormless. He couldn't remember which, but either way I'd do.

Back up to the main drag and I see the sign for The Circus, which used to be the old club where the talent show took place; well, after it got too big for the school. I haven't been in since it's been done up. It takes me a little out of my circle, but sure, what harm could that do?

I head along the upper Oldpark, and I have to say that the club doesn't look that different from the outside, except for the big sign – *The Circus*. Inside, though, I'm blown away, it looks terrific. What a transformation. Must have cost a bomb and a half. The new owner is behind the bar, but otherwise not a soul. I order a pint out of feeling sorry for the guy. On the wall behind the bar is another poster for the Talent Show. I stare at it for a while.

I've always done my impressions, ever since I was a kid. It got me all my friends, sure; well, the two, and even got the bullies to like me, or stop beating me, at least. Everybody loves it when I do them: my family, my bosses at work, the people in the street.

I order another pint out of still feeling sorry for the poor guy.

Even strangers. You know, maybe I could do it on the stage, right enough. My Jeff has always been the smart one.

I order another pint, and, I have to say, I'm starting to feel a bit good. You know what? I am going to do it. Why not?

I call Jeff. 'I'm in, I'll do the talent show,' I say.

Then Sean Connery takes over: 'I accept the mission,

Miss Moneypenny.' I laugh. 'You only said I couldn't do the voices in the house.'

I'd never done Sean before, and I'm quite good, to be fair. I think I'll use that in the show.

'Say that again,' says Jeff. 'Never mind. Get you home right now and get your Connery on. I'll be waiting upstairs.'

I don't drink the newly-poured pint. I've an intimacy schedule to follow.

The Judge

I saw the envelope from the top of the stairs. It stood out in its shocking whiteness. I was sure it was responsible for the pain I felt in my right temple. It looked cheap; the brightness designed to distract you from its lack of quality. Definitely from a multipack; imported from somewhere so far away that the shipping probably cost more than the envelope cost to make. And even from where I stood, paused, on the landing, a steadying shoulder against the wall, I could see the writing on the front was handwritten in biro. Blue. Who uses a blue biro? Honestly. People who go to bingo might – I've seen the type on TV. But on a letter? Really?

No stamp. Handwritten, hand-delivered. My stomach lurched, so I pressed the side of my face against the cool of the wall. I'd been waiting for this or something like it. It's only a matter of time before our indiscretions make themselves public. They're like weeds: ugly, pernicious little creeps pushing themselves through the cracks, causing the cracks if they have to, shattering even the hardest of surfaces.

I'd hoped for a couple more months before someone noticed the money was missing. I don't know what I was thinking taking it from the school's account. How did I think I would get away with it? It was time to pay the piper, but what with?

I wish I hadn't drunk so much at the talent show meeting last night. It was so exciting to be out. To be asked. To feel wanted again. No, that wasn't why I drank a little more than usual. It was that James, with his London ways, and that fake accent; gave me the heebie-jeebies, treating us all like we were provincial idiots because we hadn't lived in Shoreditch like him. Oh, he was patronising, asking me to be the judge, in homage to me as the original founder of the show, he said. Nonsense. He knows I still have standing in this community and my name means something. I've taught every parent, their brothers and sisters, their children. Well, the Protestants, anyway.

I got hold of myself, gripped the banister with all the energy I had in me, and made my way downstairs, one slow step at a time, one foot waiting for the other to join it before moving again. When I reached the level where sunlight blasted through the window in my front door, I felt my retinas scream and my stomach sink, but I kept going, not wanting to get dizzy. I couldn't fall; it had taken weeks to walk properly after last time. My poor ankle has never been the same.

I took a second in the hall at the bottom of the stairs to let the rough sea of last night's red wine settle. To maintain my newly-won equilibrium, I didn't bend over; instead, I sank, slowly, with my upper body straight up, like those ridiculous, rigid-looking Riverdancers. Trust the Irish to be contrary in all things – dancing stiff as pokers.

The Judge

I felt for the envelope in question. It was easily identifiable amongst the glossy, textured supermarket flyers. I rose with purpose, fearing a collapse at the knees, and stuffed the offending article into my dressing gown pocket. I looked in at the living room, but the room said *no*, quite sharply, I might add. Clearly, we weren't on speaking terms. I quite literally didn't have the stomach for a fight so I passed. Besides, experience had taught me that it's best to approach these matters when in full possession of the facts, and, right then, I didn't remember even getting home from the meeting.

The kitchen was quiet, which was a relief. There was one dish in the sink. Not sure what I'd had for dinner, but it hadn't made a mess. I looked towards the electric kettle. That I did remember. It had put on a little show the day before; the button that would not stay down to make the water boil.

'Yes, I haven't forgotten,' I said, giving it the dirtiest look. Of course, I considered whether I'd forgotten to put the button down myself, but I concluded that if I started letting things like a kettle make me doubt myself, then I really was on the road to Muckamore crazy house. Let it know who's boss, and make the punishment severe and swift, to put an end to that kind of bad behaviour right then and there, for good. Just like the kids at school. Well, before the woke nonsense.

You should have felt the atmosphere in the kitchen when I came back from the attic with the old kettle. A tin job, black bottom and all. When the electric kettle saw the old one sitting on the hob, I could have sworn I heard a little sobbing, like water bubbling; but it was too late, the damage had been done and I couldn't go back on my word. What would I be teaching it?

I popped on the old kettle and lit the gas under it. I took out the envelope and set it leaning against the biscuit barrel. From the freezer, I tried to pull a slice from a pan loaf, but they were all stuck, frozen together. I used the largest, sharpest knife I had, and was aware of the dangers, thank you – I knew my hands weren't as steady as they once were. Or me, in general. I stabbed and wiggled the blade in a tiny ridge between slices, then worked at the gap. It just wouldn't give.

Without Mum, and Abi gone to Uni in Liverpool, food got old, went off. I couldn't be bothered to cook for one. Shopping was a waste. And when I did cook, all the leftovers, they'd end up in the bin too. The fridge was always empty now, and just a few ready-meals and essentials in the freezer.

The loaf gave. I hadn't realised I'd put so much effort into it, so I was shocked to find my face slamming into the fridge door and my elbow whacking off the freezer-drawer edge. When I recovered, I looked at the knife in my hand, and my heart raced to think where it could have ended up. I was so annoyed at that knife. And then the bread. It had been the bread's fault. The danger it had put me in. The total lack of regard. I could have screamed.

I didn't bother with the second slice I'd promised myself to spite the loaf. 'See what you've done?' I shook the knife at the loaf. 'If I starve, or get sick, we'll know who to blame, won't we?'

I could have ended up in A&E again. But with a knife wound! How would I have explained that one? I was so

The Judge

angry, I pulled the loaf out of the drawer by its untwisted cellophane opening and threw the whole thing against the wall where it bounced off and onto the floor. I stamped on it; jumped on it with two feet. I slipped but managed to right myself. I hadn't expected the bread to fight back.

I took a breath and gathered myself. What had I done? What would Abi have said? She called them *episodes*. At first, she was worried; we both were, but I didn't tell her that, I told her, I'm not *Eastenders*, I don't have episodes. I knew Uni was coming up and I didn't want her doubting her decision to leave. Especially after what I'd sacrificed to get her there. Taking that money from the school. So, I kept my episodes to when she wasn't around. I held them in until I was alone. Problem was, after she left, I was alone a lot. Then, during lockdown, I was alone practically all the time. I'd hoped Abi would come home, be in my bubble, but she met a lovely boy studying geography, and they bubbled together. I didn't blame her.

I remembered the toast. Something to settle my stomach before I read that letter. When I pressed the lever on the toaster, it didn't click but popped straight back up with such force that the slice jumped up and out of the contraption.

'Really?' I said. 'Are we going to play silly buggers, now? I'm not in the mood, not this day.'

I heard my mum in the 'this day.' I even sounded like her and her broad Sandy Row accent. The elocution classes she'd sent me to worked as they were supposed to. Sometimes I put on my original working-class Belfast accent around the house like it's the false one. I imagine it's her I'm listening to.

I tried again with the lever, and the mechanism instantly

popped up. More than cheeky, it was like it was saying, "eff you, I can do whatever I want! I don't have to toast this bread just because you want me to. You don't control me!'

I'd had enough. 'Right, that's it,' I said, and pulled the plug from the wall socket, and put the toaster under my left arm like a handbag. 'You've played yourself, this day.' I heard. my mother coming from me again. I bounded up the stairs, I don't know where I got the energy, then I thought, it's from Mum.

At the landing, I took the short pole in my right hand and raised it until the hook at the tip snagged the small metal hoop in the ceiling. First time too. It knew better than to mess with me when I was in that kind of mood. I pulled, the door came towards me, and the stairs slid along the rails and clunked to a stop halfway to the ground. I released the catch at the side of the attic stairs, and the lower section slid to the floor. I rattled the ladders to make sure they were firmly planted and playing ball, then climbed up halfway, to where my head was level to the attic floor. In the dark, I could see shapes that I didn't focus on lest they became things I recognised and then have to deal with. I set the toaster on the floor and pushed it along so as not to clog up the entrance. I heard it clink against something metal, and I knew what that was. Mum's ashes.

Back on the landing, I decided not to raise the ladders back up. Something told me not to, so I reluctantly left them awkwardly blocking the way and squeezed past them, holding on to the stair-rail. I had that fitted for mum when she was getting weaker, and who knew I'd come to depend on it myself.

In the kitchen, I looked to see if my toast was ready, but

couldn't see the toaster. It was there a minute go. I could hear a low-level beeping, like a turned down alarm. It was the open freezer. I saw the loaf, and it all came back to me. It's not like I forget things forever. I just need hints. And if I don't want to remember certain things, I hide the hints.

I sat at the breakfast bar on a high stool and lifted the envelope without further ado, ripped it open, and took the letter out. Like ripping off a plaster.

It was typed, all caps, in an enormous font.

LILY,

ON THE NIGHT OF THE TALENT SHOW YOU WILL RECEIVE ANOTHER ONE OF THESE LETTERS TELLING YOU WHO TO CHOOSE AS THE WINNER OF NORTH BELFAST'S GOT TALENT. IF YOU DO AS YOU ARE ASKED YOU WILL RECEIVE HALF OF THE WINNINGS.

DETAILS GIVEN IN THE NEXT LETTER.

ANON

I heard a howling laughter, and it took a second to realise it was coming from me. I wasn't even going to say yes to judging that stupid show after last night. I'd been worried, thinking I was getting blackmailed, that someone had discovered the money missing. The prize money could fix everything. I had always intended to give it back. That's right. That was it. I'd only borrowed it from the school account. And then the pandemic hit, and I panicked, during one of my episodes, and resigned.

I'll find a way of getting that money back into the

account. Maybe then, with nothing to hide, I could make a play for my old job. I could get my old life back. Get *me* back.

What is that beeping?

The Comedian

'SHORT BACK AND sides,' I say, looking at him in the mirror.

I speak slowly when I talk to Mohammed, or Wee Mo, as the locals have christened him. I do it so he's more likely to understand me, of course, but mostly so I don't have to repeat myself. Since lockdown, saying things out loud has become exhausting. Not a great scenario for a performer.

One of the reasons I come to the Turkish barbers is because Mohammed's English is terrible. I'm not forced into those inane conversations, having to endure one of their holiday monologues; trapped in the chair, a captive audience for these people. He's happy to cut in silence, unlike every other barber round here. By the way, when I say 'these people', I don't mean foreigners, I mean barbers and hairdressers. I'm not racist; I hate everyone equally. If anything, I take his side over our ones.

The reason I've come to Mohammed's today is that poster in his window for North Belfast's Got Talent. I'm not superstitious really, but I thought I'd get my hair cut in this chair with the poster behind me. Ten-thousand smackaroonies. My name on every note.

Poor Mohammed has put his place up for sale. Cliftonville Circus was dying: a bookies, a butchers, a chippie, and a solicitors. In comes Mohammed and opens up his wee barbers. High quality, multicultural; a new worldly way for us closed-up North Belfastians. Cheap as chips too – seven quid for hair and beard – throws in your eyebrows and sets your ears on fire for free. That's some way of getting rid of ear hair. Who came up with that? That would be the Turks, I guess.

Here in Northern Ireland, we were closed off all those years because of the Troubles. No tourists, no visiting bands, or culture, or comedy. Left simmering in our own juices for far too long. It reduced us like a stock; too strong in flavour, we needed to be diluted; added to. And that's been happening since the Troubles ended. And the people are changing, the place is changing. Who'd have thought there would ever be a Turkish barbers on Cliftonville Circus? And a new bar opened by a Soho nightclub owner.

Mohammed did so well, not one but two other barbers opened up on the Circus. One of them, another Turkish barbers, but with two guys from Ardoyne. Now Mohammed's is up for sale. There's not enough business for three. I wouldn't be surprised if he's been told to frig off. I know it's all 'the Troubles is over', and it mostly is, but the paramilitaries are still here and about. I haven't heard anything specific, but I know words go in ears, and that's all I'm saying. Soon I'll have to suffer local barbers, or head into town; either way, I'll be at their mercy. I like it the other way around. Me on stage and my prey in the audience.

The Comedian

I've always been funny. Are you born with it, I wonder? A gift from the comedy gods? Or is it the jewel that is formed over time. Nature or nurture? I was the kid at school who would joke around all the time. I was smart, but I just couldn't translate that into the kind of smart that got you good grades and into the good books of teachers. The odd one fell for my funny, usually a female teacher, with a twinkle in her eye. In secondary school, there weren't so many female teachers, so I went hard on the classmates. I learned quickly that the more anti-learning, anti-school, anti-teacher I became, the more popular I was.

It's an albatross. Having a talent. For a start, round here can be so grim that it's hard to get motivated to write, be creative, or find anything at all funny. By far the worst thing is, people torture you at parties and in the pub when you've told them you're a comic. They're like: 'Tell us a joke then, mate. Go on, go on,' and if you don't, they get annoyed, and can even turn nasty. It's like being funny means you have a public duty to entertain people. I say to them, 'What do you do?' and they're like, 'I'm an accountant,' and I'm like, 'Here, add this up, go on, go on, here's my receipts, put them on a spreadsheet while you're on the dance floor.' It's a job. I don't want to work when I'm socialising.

It's become so bad I rarely go out with my old mates anymore. They're trying to be funny all the time. ALL of the time. Drives me insane. Banter. I hate banter! Batter – that's what I'd like to do, batter them until they stop trying to be funny and just have normal conversations. Nothing winds me up more. Every time we'd meet, they'd try to outdo each other with the quips, but they're mostly just repeating the same bad jokes over and over again. There is no crime greater than the crime of unfunny. In my head, I'm five jokes ahead of them; I know what that one is going to say and how that one is going to reply, and at the same time I'm rewriting their attempts at humour so that they are actually funny. Leave it to the experts and stop trying! I mean, one of my mates is a bomb disposal expert – you wouldn't have me sitting with him saying 'Here, give me a go at that one,' just because I saw James Bond do it in a movie.

That's not all I have to deal with. Since I did that those few Instagram live posts during lockdown, people seem to know my jokes. Sometimes when I'm out now, at a club, say, a group of guys will come up to me, and these gangs don't care – you could be in the middle of your John Travolta on the dance floor – I'm more *Pulp Fiction* John than *Saturday Night Fever* John – and there they'll appear: 'Tell us the one about the man, you know, yer man. Ah, wait to hear this, lads, it's absolutely brilliant.' You will not get rid of them, and they won't take no for an answer, but when you actually go to the bother of telling their favourite joke, the mouthy guy (it's always a man) will shout out the punchline before you get there, and laugh hysterically at himself.

At my last try-out night, a punter shouted out one of my punchlines. What they don't realise is that their little moment in the limelight is ruining a joke you've been weaving in and out of your set while you've held the audience in the palm of your hands for, oh, ten minutes, all leading up to that precious payoff, and bam! *They* get the laugh. *Your* laugh. The one you've spent months creating and they stole so cheaply. What's more, I'm sure the audience assumed this genius worked it out himself; that he was ten steps ahead of me, that I was read like a cheap Christmas-stocking joke book.

I lost the audience then. There was no coming back from something like that. They lost their trust in me. The comedian was no longer the funniest one in the room. I could have gone in on the comedy cuckoo; hit him with my best put-downs, had the room laugh at him. But the audience would have thought I was only going after him because I was caught fair and square, and the harder I'd go at him, the more it'd look like it hurt me.

'Shorter?' asks Mohammed, pulling a clump of my hair towards the ceiling, two fingers like scissors showing the extra inch he could take off. Mohammed laughs because he knows I won't like it shorter. He knows the way I like my hair: that extra bit of length at the top that covers my widow's peak. I'm going to miss him. I'll have to break a new guy in, and it's a pain.

'You. Cut. Me. I. Cut. You,' I say, and run my thumb along my neck. He laughs.

I thought there'd be this camaraderie in comedy. A brotherhood of gags. We'd be sitting in the green room sharing jokes and telling stories, only breaking out of it to go on stage and do legendary sets. In reality, it was just egos trying to outdo each other. Who's the funniest? Who could top the laugh before? Which I get, of course – sharpening our wits, etcetera, like gladiators in the comedy colosseum preparing to fight – but there was no appreciation of how good *your* joke was; just bettering your joke. There were one of two who sat and watched us competing who looked miserable as sin. They'd hardly say hello. What was strange was those same guys would get up on stage and become this charming, funny, lovable, smiling presence. It would come across as so genuine. It was like a switch; offstage, the lights went off. It was like unless there's money in the meter then there's no electricity, no light, no star. I get that with punters, and ordinary people in your life, but not with other comedians, I mean, this is our tribe.

I'd almost given up on the whole game. Northern Ireland is just too small for a talent like mine. They don't really get me. There's a few gigs. And you see the same comedians all the time, and they get all the work. The promoters have their favourites too. You see all the young ones, sucking up to them, kissing the ring. Well, I don't kiss the ring. I want my own ring. The few MCs saying my jokes just aren't funny enough, they've just got it in for me. They think they're great but they can't even write a joke.

MCs are mostly those comedians who can come up with stuff there and then or read the newspaper that day and respond to that. But, if you notice, they're not the proper act, not the stars. Why? Because, well – and I know this will sound harsh – it's not as great a talent. There, I've said it. It's not the same as a crafted joke, put together like a classic watch. A joke is an engine, finely tuned with hours of testing to reach perfection. A joke for all time, one that you can use in any room with any demographic, and all those moving parts will click, one after the other, until the hands move, the bells chime. That laugh – you could set your watch to it.

The Comedian

When I saw the poster for the talent show, it was like the comedy Zeus sent a lightning bolt from the sky and struck my funny bone. The jokes came pouring out of me. To think I'd almost given up on comedy. I called up the old gang and arranged a drink in the new club that's hosting the show. The guys were a bit off when we met up. They didn't seem in a laughing mood, even though I was on fire with my new material. Maybe they were sulking because I hadn't seen them for a while, or maybe they're just jealous.

The talent show has brought that love for laughter back. Phoenix from the pandemic flame. That prize money can get me everything I need to launch a career over the water, where it matters. My big shot. I have it all worked out. I'm going to make a showreel: all my best jokes; the set of all sets. Not filmed on my iPhone like the muppets here; I'd have £10,000 to make a classy one, with a proper videographer. I've asked that James fella at his new club if I can film it there, and he said he'd give me a good deal. I'll send a short section to all the top agents in London, get them excited. I could even book a venue off Soho somewhere and do *An Audience With*. That prize money will more than cover it, surely. This is it. I can feel it.

Netflix special, here I come.

The Medium

Sam asked me what will I do at the talent show? And I told her, I will spill all the tea on the life hereafter. I will give them a glimpse into the new lives of their loved ones who have transitioned to heavenly bodies.

I'm here to do the Big Man's work and if I can bring more people into Our Father's fold by sharing my gifts, then I'm complete. I want to ensure eternal happiness for as many of the people as I can.

I tell my followers: 'As long as you are with me, your future is safe as houses.' I tell them: 'A happy afterlife is guaranteed.' I tell them: 'You are already angels; you just haven't died yet.' It brings great comfort to most when I tell them that, and to those it doesn't, I say: 'Ask yourself why? There's one reason only – you haven't purchased real estate in the afterlife.'

My loyal and dedicated followers are on their way to being Heavenly Homeowners; a name I'm in the process of trademarking and have already designed the t-shirts for. I know – I never stop; but those spirits just won't let me sleep, the chatty wee chipmunks, so I have to put my mind on God's work or the Evil One will have his way with me.

My wee 'investors in the afterlife': they are God's favoured ones, because I have a dedicated line to Heaven and talk to God Himself about each and every one of them. Daily. And there's not many who have that power or have their permanent slot in God's day-planner.

I've actually started my own Hotline to Heaven, so those who subscribe to my social media channels can talk to God themselves – behind a paywall, out of necessity. When they call, they get me on the other end – not because I think I'm God – woah, hold on, no way. I like to think of myself as God's switchboard operator: I put people through to Him; some have even heard God talk back to them, which I find highly unlikely, as God doesn't talk to just anyone – it would be delusional to think he would. Unfortunately, it's par for the course for some reason, to attract that sort, in my calling – although, I hate that phrase. It's a job, a profession, and, as I tell my congregation, like any other job, it needs a wage. Who works for nothing? No-one. Anyway, attracting the unhinged – it's what happens when you're close to God, and I think that's the work of Him Downstairs. He's like a union leader trying to get the workers to strike.

I tell mine: 'To follow me is to secure your place with God.' It's like putting a down payment on a home for your future, and property in Heaven is always going up in price; there's never been a property crash in the hereafter. The older you get, the less time you have to pay for that beach-front property in the sky, so get to paying that mortgage off asap. God forbid you'd die and you've only saved enough for a house on a rough estate, or God even more forbid, a pokey wee flat in a tower block.

People have come to me, and they've said, 'Malcolm, I've no money this month; if I pay you, I won't be able to pay my real mortgage.' I tell them: 'Don't start me on a *real* mortgage. You think this short time on Earth is real? That this is the real life?' I tell them: 'We are only being tested for the real life. The afterlife *is* the real life and the eternal one, don't forget.' I tell them: 'If you have to sacrifice now for everlasting luxury, then that's what you do, unless you're a fool. Are you a fool?' I ask them. 'There's only one pension you need to be paying into, and that's God's pension plan, and right now it's on offer at £99 a month.'

I will have to put that up soon, what with the energy crisis and interest rates going up. I say, 'God's inflation is good inflation; it gets you higher and higher, and that is, as we all know, closer to Him Upstairs.'

Some people don't like what I have to say. They don't like me because they don't like the truth. Well, Jesus didn't get anywhere by telling people what they *wanted* to hear; he told them what they *needed* to hear. Vilified by everyone: the church, the state, the people. So, when the haters come at me, saying their church condemns me, what I do, I say, 'Thank you.' I say, 'Then you hate Jesus and me both.' There are those that would say that I shouldn't compare myself to Jesus, and I laugh. I tell them: 'If God didn't want me to compare myself to Jesus, why would he have made me so like him?' I tell them: 'I don't think I'm Jesus Himself, God forbid, no,' and I apologise; not to them, but to God, if I ever misspoke to suggest that. I am not Jesus, no. I'm like him, yes; plain for all, who have eyes, to see. I tell them: 'Think of me like Jesus's brother: like him, but

The Medium

with his own place in the family.' Some might even prefer him to his brother, but that's not for me to say.

It is exhausting being me. Taking care of everyone. Always putting myself last. I finally got myself an assistant, after being coaxed by all and everyone. Even God Himself had a word with me. He berated me for working my fingers to the bone. He said, 'Malcolm, even I had a day of rest.' So, I finally relented and got Sam. I mean, you can hardly say no to God Himself. The arrogance.

She's doing it for free, Sam, God love her. Well, not for free, as I've given her a discount on her monthly subscription. I mean, working for me equals everlasting life; well, as long as you stay working for me – I can't say what would happen if you stopped.

It's a no-brainer for her, though. Sadly, there are some people with no brains in this world, but thankfully not Sam. It's amazing what's happening to her right in front of my eyes. I've seen it happen before, so it's not me imagining it: people actually get smarter when they spend time with me. They start to think like me, start to say things I would say – it's incredible – like just being around me elevates them to a higher place.

Sam's not quite there yet and, God bless her, she is dull. I was thinking, 'I'm sure God has His reason for making her that way,' and what do you know – God did. Last night, when we were walking up the Westland Road, I was finding it so hard to listen to her, through no fault of my own. Sam's a wee dote, honest she is, but she's a sleeping tablet. She starts talking, and I struggle to stay awake. And I thought: Sam = sleeping tablet. They could use her as an anaesthetic in operating theatres. I knew that was too big to start off with, so when we got back to the flat, we made a podcast for insomniacs. I wrote the words, obviously, but I got Sam to record the vocal. I listened to it myself, and I went to sleep within seconds.

I'm rolling the sleep podcast out tonight on my Facebook Live readings session. I need to find a name for it, but I'm not worried; I've sent the spirits a voice note, and they will get back to me later. When I think of it, I could wean people off those harmful sleeping tablets if we can make it a success. What do I mean *if*? *If*? Listen to me! That's Him Downstairs whispering in my ear. Of course it will be a success. And think of the future. Removing the need for those toxic drugs and gasses they use for operations. Using my words, my prayers, like a form of spiritual hypnotism, not the Derren Brown, end-of-pier show kind.

Last night, it stuck me: this could single-handedly save the NHS, an idea like this. Then, suddenly, I felt weak. Drained. Sam and I were on our way to The Circus. One of my spiritual children, Rachel, had told me all about the local talent show; she's going to be a magician's assistant, bless. Now, my first reaction was I'd never be involved in something that grossly commercial. Me using my gifts for entertainment, for money. But, when I heard the amount, £10,000, I had to stop, think of the amount of God's work I could do with a sum of money like that.

I was still struggling, even knowing the above. It wasn't until we passed the golf course. I saw how busy it was. There must have been something on in the clubhouse: a christening, a wedding, a charity event, maybe. I thought about the new club, The Circus. I thought about the coincidences I'd told Rachel to look out for, which she'd found everywhere, and I thought, 'Stop neglecting yourself; you need to look out for your own coincidences.' If I made it work for her, gave her the answers and opened her eyes, why wouldn't I do it for myself? Surely, God and the universe would present for me. I looked at the golf clubhouse; it was a club, and the talent show was in a club. Then Sam reminded me that golf was played with a club. I mean, it was pretty obvious, wasn't it? But still I had resistance.

We continued our stroll up to The Circus. I realised we'd crossed that invisible border where the Protestant road had become Catholic. We passed the new barbers, and onto Cliftonville Circus, and that's when everything just went into a whole other realm. Now, this was a weird one, even for me. I heard a rumbling. Like an earthquake was brewing below. I felt it come from the deep. Up and through me. Normally things descend upon me, so this was something else. And there was water. Rushing. Underneath. 'Run with me,' it said. So I did. I ran across Oldpark Road, car horns blaring. I ran across Alliance Avenue, then down its left side. It was behind the houses. The fourth house down. The gates were open, so I ran up the drive, along the side wall, and across the back garden to the hedges. There. Behind was a small stream. The water. It had something to tell me. But it wasn't for me. It was for whoever lived in this house. It was their parents who had passed. They must travel on the water and leave this place.

I walked back across the grass to the window at the back of the house. I saw a room empty of furniture except for a mattress on the floor. Sam had caught up with me. She was talking to the next-door neighbour at the gate.

'Who lives here?' I asked.

'Yer James one,' she said. 'The one running the talent show.'

I had my sign from God. I should take part in the talent show. And I had a message for James.

The Drag Queen

It's pronounced Dee-lor-ez, not *Dul*-lor-es. There's nothing *dull* about this drag queen, honey. Mysterious, some might say – who is she under all that make-up, the fabulous hair and glamorous dresses? *They seek me here, they seek me there*; I'm like the Lilac Pimpernel.

Too young to get the reference? I can see it in your eyes. I'd explain it but I'm nearly dead, love, I don't have the time to waste. Forgive me, I'm running low on sugar. I'm not diabetic; sweet things are my attempt at counteracting all the bitterness inside me. You liked that one, didn't you? It's the same with the drag shows; the cheekier we are, the edgier, the more risqué, the more the audience loves it. Especially the straights – can't get enough. And the ones who hate us? Well, we know all about those who shout the loudest – and that's scientifically proven. You can write that down with an exclamation mark!

I was referencing *The Scarlet Pimpernel*. Oh, I must have watched those black and white shows hundreds of times, back in the olden days, when this queen was just a twinkle behind my alter ego's unlashed eyes. There I'd be in my mum's bedroom, in her dresses and heels; a right mess, let me tell you. And look at me now: a beautiful, glamorous, sophisticated lady – of the dockyards. It's that clash that brings the cash. Yes, that's mine and, yes, you can use it.

The Scarlet Pimpernel was the first superhero, you know, and that's from the mouth of Mr Marvel, Stan Lee, himself. The character was camp and unthreatening during the day, a figure not taken seriously by society, but his alter ego was loved and feared; took on his enemies and outwitted them all. A rebel with a cause. Can you see where I'm going here? Yes, basically drag queens are superheroes – just another reason why kids love us, now that we no longer need to live in the shadows.

Are you getting all this? I don't see you taking notes. Ah, phones. Is there nothing they can't do these days? I still have my old one that barely does a thing but text and call. The other drag queens laugh at me, until they see how long my battery lasts.

Now listen treacle, I will go off on all sorts of tangents, so you will have to keep hold of my reins. I could put a pair on, if you ask me nicely. I did wear some last Christmas Eve and literally pranced up and down Union St. I had a flashing red nose and everything. I like to put the *rude* in *Rud*-olph.

Where is James? I'm sorry, I'm sure he'll be here soon. I guess you're just stuck with fabulous old me. Poor you. A private audience with a Belfast legend. You'll be able to dine out on this one for years to come, Sonny Jim.

That's what we called James back in school – well, Jimmy to be precise. Who'd have thought he'd appear back on the scene, arriving home after thirty-odd years away. He'd hang out with my little gang at school sometimes, even though we were the freaks, the fruits, the rejects, the weirdos. We were the exiled, so we had no choice but to be on the outside; but he chose to be there, when he had the charm and the looks and straightness to be with *them*. The norms.

He was one of the rare kids who wasn't embarrassed being seen with us. The rest were worried that being seen with us tainted them, that they'd be rejected and mocked too. There were some who talked to us when no-one else was watching, but James never passed us by without a hello and a hug. That takes a special kind of character. To stand against the crowd. To stand up. To take up for people when you don't need to. And that's why I agreed to do this for him. I'm standing up for him now. I'm a superhero, remember.

Don't be putting this in your article – I don't want there to be any talk of the difficulties he's been having. You've heard, of course. Look, he was always going to face resistance from the locals, but what a lot of them don't know, or have forgotten, is that he's a local too. He's from Ardoyne, for God's sake! Even though he did go to the Belfast Royal Academy; not something a kid of his persuasion did back then. Which, when I think about it, probably made him a bit of an outcast with the other Catholics he lived beside.

So, you see, he was living a lie in our school, every day, like me – we were hiding our true selves to stay safe. In a school that was for well-to-do Protestants, he was a working-class Catholic. He wasn't the only one, but one of the few. I knew because on the way home from school one day, I saw him from the bus window, as it turned round Cliftonville Circus. James had taken off his tie, and he was carrying his blazer inside out, with the school badge hidden. If people knew your school, they knew your religion, and that could get you killed.

It was when I saw James take a left down Alliance Avenue, I knew. There were streets we Protestants wouldn't walk down.

Now, some things have changed. In Ballysillan Park, across from me, I've seen some Catholics, younger ones, about your age, walking their dogs. I suppose nobody would know their background, but I recognised them from the working men's clubs I do my shows at. I think it's brilliant myself, us moving forward; but I'd be a liar if I didn't say it makes me a little uncomfortable. There was a time when we had a chunk of Ardoyne, but no more. *And* the Oldpark Road, from more-or-less Cliftonville Circus up; they're creeping up, street by street. There's talk of one or two in my street. They just have so many kids, don't they? Now, as I say, I don't mind, I think it's wonderful we're all moving on, and I don't care what anyone is, and I don't care what you are, honestly. That's all in the past.

Where is James? I'm getting annoyed now. Let's see if he's been in touch. Pass my handbag, would you be a love? Did I catch you looking at my legs? Eyes up here, dear! Cheeky. There's my glasses. Aren't they fabulously over-the-top? Very Dame Edna Everage, don't you think? Quite the inspiration she was. Christ, the night – not

Dame Edna as well? Right, get a pen and paper and write down these references. Make a list. Get yourself educated.

Text from my mother . . . text from a little *liaison dangereuse* – put that on your movie list, for Glenn Close and her frocks. Oh, here: '*Sorry, beautiful, something's come up. I know you'll shine like the star you are.*'

How can I stay annoyed at a charmer like that? Anyway, let's start proper. You're sure this is recording?

Let me warm up – *do-re-mi-fa-so-la-ti-do*. Have you seen *The Sound of Music*? Sweet baby cheeses. In the name of Babybel and all that's good in the world. The list, child, put it on the list! Stop watching football and *Love Island* – though do watch *Real Housewives*. I'm pitching 'Real Housewives of Ballysillan' at the mo, if you know anyone in the biz.

James came back from London, where he was huge, darling, simply *huge* in the property market. Owned half of Soho, as I hear it, not that he said that to me; it's not his style to brag – far too classy. Even with all that success, the lure of home was too great. Who knows, I might have had a little something to do with that, but hush-hush. Well, James sold up and is now bringing a bit of the West End to North Belfast. And I think it's wonderful he bought over the old club. I know it's ruffled a few feathers – not the ones on this dress, honey, they're fake; and rather fabulous, don't you think?

Those complaining on Facebook, or Fakebook, as I call it, are just that – fake. They're the dinosaurs who just don't want Belfast to move on. If they had their way, they'd still have men in one room and women in the other. Hard to believe it was like that when I was a kid. In that respect, working men's clubs have moved with the times – sure, they've me doing gay bingo in West Belfast and everything. The haters can just suck it up.

At the end of the day, if that old place was making money, it wouldn't have been up for sale and, yes, I get that it's another loss for us, another Protestant bar gone. The club was once surrounded by Protestant people living in Protestant streets; it's now all Catholics on one side and us on the other. My James has zero interest in all that stuff; he's lived in London all these years, with every nationality under the sun in every street, he says. Wouldn't you know his luck, though, both sides here are against the place. One for where it's been, and one for where it's going. It's hard to win in Belfast.

That's why I convinced James to bring back North Belfast's Got Talent. Throw the locals a bone, I said; get them in, and hopefully win them over. I've agreed to be the hostess with the mostest. This area's never seen anything like it before. It'll certainly be the first time I've done drag on a North Belfast stage. It's like my second coming out, if you like. People round my way don't know my secret identity. To them I'm the mild-mannered gentleman who likes to read; the polite dog-owner who walks his teacup Yorkie to the local shops for a little chat and a nosy. But that anonymity is all going to change soon.

So, yes, we want everyone to come – all ages, all religions, all genders, all sexualities, all talents. Sign up soon. Write that.

Do you like this new dress? Every sequin hand-sewn. Done by a little seamstress who makes her daughters Irish

Dancing costumes down the Cliftonville. I met her in the butcher's many moons ago and we've been friends ever since. I wish I could do it myself. Don't get me wrong – I can design, use the sewing machine too, a lot of things, in fact, but needle work? Have you seen these hands? That's why I hide them with long gloves. *And* how I got my drag name. I started as Delores de Beauvoir – the surname after Simone; I had aspirations back then. Some people might have said pretentions, but they were just jealous of my intelligence. Not heard of De Beauvoir? Put her on the list; raise yourself, child.

Anyway, the name didn't last, especially after I started doing the clubs. I didn't wear gloves back then, and a nasty queen took one look at me and said, 'They're the hands of a docker'. Next thing I knew, Dockyard Delores was out there, and the name stuck. I should thank that evil queen, she did me a favour; it became part of my act and made me into the icon I am today.

I bumped into James in the street, would you believe. I recognised him right away. The same blue eyes, like a movie star. I had stared at them long enough as a love-struck teenager. Don't you be putting that in, that's between me and you. Of course, I said hello and, well, I'd heard about his predicament. The business only new and failing, everyone against him . . . so I offered to help.

James is coaxing me to reveal my drag career. I mean he's right – with RuPaul and all that *Drag Race* stuff – sure the young people love it and it's all over the TV. What's there to fear? Well, the way they came after that young drag queen in Belfast for reading stories to kids: death threats, and shameful accusations of unspeakable things;

all because he's wearing a dress. That is what actually made my mind up. I'm going to say it out loud and be proud – on stage – whip the wig off and do my own take on a gender reveal!

I stand with drag queens! And I'll be doing gigs with that wee drag queen, and let them come for him and they'll see what these docker's hands can do.

The Gymnast

Hello Dearest,

How are you? Do you miss me? I'm sorry I don't write enough. I have been thinking too much and it has made me not know what to say. More time should make it easier but it makes things worse. What to tell you and how? And what not to tell you. So, I decided not to think and to write instead. I am writing to you in the English to practise. You were always better at it than me. How ironic that you were the one who had no interest in leaving home. 'Ironic', is good, yes?

You ask me what it is like in Belfast, and about the people and to tell you everything about me. That is a lot. I will try.

First, the sky is too low. It is obvious to me why the people here are sometimes cross and sad. How would you feel if there were days when you could reach up and touch the clouds? It is a city being pressed on by the sky. It's like we are in a pot, being cooked and someone is putting on the lid to make us bubble and boil up.

It's so strange to me that people in Belfast don't look up.

Is it the falling sky they are afraid to look at? It reminds of the book when we were at school – was he a chicken afraid the sky was falling on him? You will remember, you always remember everything, you are so good. Maybe it is the same everywhere, not looking up, but I notice it in Belfast more. I looked on the internet, it said that looking down is connected to being depressed, that if you are feeling sad you should make yourself look up and you will feel happier. I can't remember why.

I think people in Belfast can be sad. I think the people should be told to look up. If they looked up, they'd see how beautiful Belfast is and how lucky they are. Is this why looking up makes people happier? The internet sites I looked at about Belfast, before I moved here, never talked about hills. I had heard about the hills surrounding Rome but Belfast has them too.

I have walked up Divis and Cavehill. You can go to the Castle – yes Belfast has a castle too – and walk up through the forest behind. You can't go into the cave Cavehill is named after because it is high up but you could once. There were wooden steps, or a platform, or a ladder, my memory isn't so good today. I am distracted. I am writing to you to calm myself.

A man stood on a platform and took money at the cave. Yes, I saw an old photo inside the castle. I saw another photo there of a big diamond that was found on cave hill and people would pay to come and see it. It wasn't real though. The man made a fool out of everyone. Why do men do that?

Even when you are in the city centre, between the

buildings you can see the hills behind. It is strange to see these modern buildings with nature playing peek-a-boo like you do with babies. Sometimes it feels like I am in a movie set, or on a stage, and they have forgotten to pull up the backdrop so two movies are mixed. I think Belfast is two movies at the same time.

Have you seen any good movies lately? I don't have a TV. At night, sometimes I find a film on my phone, but I am so tired I fall asleep after five minutes. I don't have much energy these days. I thought from work but now, maybe, I don't know.

When I walk down from Oldpark Road Tony's house, did I tell you about him, last time? Oldpark Road Tony likes very sparkly clothes that are for women but I never seen him wear them outside or even inside his house. Not clothes like women would wear in the street but I think at a fancy ball in the old days. Very glamorous but maybe not so nice. I think maybe he wears them for shows but he doesn't mention so I don't mention. I don't want you to think I am nosy, but I can't help being in people's business with my work.

What else? You do not have to take your shoes off to go into someone's house here which is crazy, especially when I just clean the floor and they walk in with their shoes. They must have too much money. Also, they have many children – sometimes seven or eight even. What else? After they meet you only once they call you by your first name! And you must follow the rules with a queue; I have seen a grown man fight with fists over what they call 'bunking'. They wouldn't like these queues at home.

I was telling you about going down from Oldpark Road

Tony's, it is a steep hill, and maybe for two streets only, you can see, over the houses on the Cliftonville Road past the Circus, one of their famous cranes. They call these cranes Samson and Goliath, like a pet name, I think. I don't know which one it is that you can see from there.

These cranes were for the once famous ship yards. I didn't know the Titanic was built in Belfast; this is amazing to me. I said to Alliance Ave James and he said even he didn't know that either until he heard that the Titanic Museum was being built. How could you be from the city and not know?

Alliance Ave James left many years ago because of the Trouble, which was very bad and many people left and also many people didn't come to visit or to live, like me. He didn't know about the Titanic, but he did know Oldpark Road Tony who passed on my number to work at his. They went to school together many, many years ago when I was only young. This is strange to think about but when you are grown up the age gap doesn't matter so much.

Are you still mad with me? You know I love you, but I had to leave. I didn't want to stay there my whole life. I would have been so sad, and I would have blamed you, and then where would we have been? Like your parents? I don't say that to hurt you, but you know it's true. Now, I look at the mess I'm in and I wish I'd never left you.

What I love most about here is how close you are to the water. When I am not working, I go to Holywood. Not where the stars are, and the movies, of course. It still makes me laugh, though, when I say, 'I am going to Holywood today.' It is said 'Hollywood', like the one in America, but it is spelt like its history – Holy-wood – for the woods behind a monastery. People in Belfast don't seem to know this either. Which I don't understand. It is strange what they choose to remember here. But I like it. Maybe because I am strange too.

In Holywood I walk along the water. If you like, you can walk on the sand. You can take your shoes off and walk in the water. You can watch the ferries and cruise ships come and go. It is not the sea. It is called the Belfast Lough. Alliance Avenue James took me there, the first time, and we walked all the way to Bangor. It is such a beautiful town, built around the waterfront.

I love being near the water. It is all I can think of to do when I have time off from work. It's not easy to make friends when the language doesn't come quickly from your mouth, and in Belfast they speak so fast. Alliance Avenue James says they had to say things quickly because they were always running away from the bullets and bombs. He can be funny sometimes. He also lets me borrow his car. He says it is an 'old banger', which is also funny. He is one of the few people I can understand here, because he lived in London for many years, so his accent is not so Belfast. I think maybe he is my friend, although I clean his house, so it's hard to tell. I think he is lonely like me. People don't seem to like him either. They treat him like a foreigner although he is from here. I think maybe you can be a foreigner in your own city. I think I was when I lived at home.

I walk in a place called the Waterworks, which is near where I live on the Cliftonville Road. It has two lakes – one that looks natural, with an island and fishermen in boats; the other, like an outdoor pool, but it is not a pool for swimming. If you walk towards the Westland Road, along the natural-looking lake, it is pretty to see the hungry swans, but if you look up – the view!

You see the hill they call the sleeping giant. His face in profile, lying down. I go here when the house is too noisy. The banging, the shouting, the throbbing of the music. Last night, the police came across the road to raid a house for drugs. I didn't mind all this when I first moved here, but now I have so much to think about.

It would be odd to people here if I told them I had never seen the sea before I came. They are an island here, nowhere more than sixty miles from the sea. Can you imagine? I told Alliance Ave James that some people say my home, Czechia, means the dry place. I told him about the droughts that uncovered the hunger stones in the river near Děčín. 'When you see me, weep,' one said. Is this why water makes me so happy?

When I saw Bangor, I said, 'I would like to live here'. Alliance Avenue James laughed at me, which I didn't like. He cannot think about people's feelings sometimes. I have been saving every penny. I don't go out to the bar, or the club, or buy nice things. I save it all.

Alliance Avenue James lives alone in a big empty house. He has bought an old bar that I am cleaning for him. The wages are too good. He is silly with his money. Not like a good Czech boy. Not like you. He will have a competition there, and he said I should try. What can I do? Maybe some gymnastics, like I used to do at school only. He said he could help me win. We could share the money. I will admit to you that I thought about it. A deposit for a flat, and some left for furniture.

I even went to the shopping centre and tried on some sports clothes yesterday. I noticed my belly was a shape it's never been. I turned to my profile, put my hand on the little bump and I knew. Do you know what I am not telling you?

When I got back to my room, I lay down on the bed and for the first time I was glad it was a small bed. Like when I was a kid. I wanted to feel small again. I tucked the sheets and blankets in very tight and worked myself under them, feet first. I wanted to feel sealed in like I was in a cocoon.

I looked out my bedroom window and saw Cave Hill, like a painting in a frame. I saw the sleeping giant lying there, lying there like me. With me. When I dreamed, I was in the water at Holywood. I was floating. Like the water was holding me. The waves came like arms; they held me, carried me, like a baby. I saw the sleeping giant, his head the land, his body the water. I woke up sad. Like the people here are sometimes.

I want to come home. But if I do, when you see me, I think you will weep.

The Organiser

It started the way things always start for me: that buzz, fizzing through my body, and me feeling invincible; ready to take on, and over, the world. It has ended like everything else in my life has: a complete flippin' shit show. The finale of North Belfast's Got Talent was pandemonium. I named my club well when I called it The Circus, but turns out The Titanic would have been more apt. That place has sunk for good. I bet the search parties are out looking for me right now. Someone's bound to have connected me going missing to Rachel disappearing.

Is it because I went out of my way to step on all those pavement cracks when I was a child? The bolshie wee bugger that I was. Maybe it was that time in Dublin when I didn't buy the bunch of lucky heather from the old woman in O'Connell Street. Am I being punished because I ran away from that job in Australia, leaving them high and dry and in the red? Or is it that I did it all and never looked back? But you're not supposed to look back, right? Pillars of salt and all that.

Rachel is looking out of the passenger-side window,

The Organiser

hail tapping aggressively against it. She's shivering, and her breath is making brief clouds on the glass. The heating isn't working in the old banger Sean sold me when I first got here. I did only pay three hundred quid for it, so it's to be expected.

Rachel looks like she's somewhere else. I thought she'd be elated: ditching that husband, getting revenge, finally breaking free. All that Beyoncé stuff. This is her first time. Leaving does get easier, if you make a habit of it, like I have. But it catches up with you eventually. Look at me coming back home after all these years. This time I'm staying. I'm going to face the music.

Rachel had to do it this way. By all accounts, her Frank is barking mad; a real sicko. He's probably still scratching his head, wondering what happened. Maybe that's what she's thinking about in this quiet moment.

It was supposed to be different this time. For me. All my ducks were in a row. I'd thought of everything; I was sure of it. I had the money. I had history in Belfast; I came from Ardoyne, for Christ's sake, knew the place and the people. Still had some old friends living here too, for back-up; not that I'd kept in touch much, but I checked them out online now and again, from a distance. My parents might have passed, but Seán was still alive and kicking, and even if he wasn't quite talking to me, everything can be repaired in life, right? I was coming home, to stay, to finally settle down. For good. I hadn't thought of that phrase like that before. For good. To do good. It's true. I really did want to give something back to Belfast, where I grew up. And somewhere, in the back of my head, returning to the place I first ran away from; I think I saw a reset, back to the start to change my ways. Make a new path, erasing all that had been before.

I'll admit, I was naïve about here. I believed the narrative about Belfast having changed. To me, it sounded like the gentrification of the ghettoes of London where the arty, the immigrants, the outcasts and the poor all lived in relative harmony. Then came the middle-class, first-time buyers loving the edge, the vibrancy of those communities, the cultural mix that made it trendy – but, mostly, loving the affordable mortgages. Next thing you know, *Vogue* is doing a feature on the area and the people who made the place what it was can no longer afford to live there. I thought Belfast was like that. Most of it. It had been rehabilitated in financial eyes. No more bombs, no more IRA and UDA, and no more Troubles; oh no, now it was all *Game of Thrones* Tours and the Titanic Museum.

When everything fell apart in London, losing all that money invested in Dubai, Belfast was the first place that sprung to mind. A short jump over the water, hardly an hour on the plane. The property, laughably cheap. I still can't believe I was able to buy our old family home, and for a sum of money you couldn't buy a toilet with in London – or Dublin for that matter. My God, the price of everything down there; I thought London was bad.

Selling up in London made me enough money to buy our old house outright. If only I'd stopped there, kept the rest and taken early retirement; put some aside for a rainy day. But no, I had to buy that club. They're probably wrecking the place this very minute. They'll be thinking I've scarpered with the prize money. Thing is, there never was any prize money. I'd sunk all I had into renovating the building and making it into The Circus: 'A bit of the West End in North Belfast'. Well, turned out most people didn't want that.

There were those who just wanted things to stay the way they were, but that wasn't possible because things are changing here. Then, those that wanted something new couldn't agree on what that was. I offered them something forward-thinking; taking a leap into the future, to catch up with the rest of the world. But hardly anyone got on board. I guess that's what happens when you're ahead of your time.

And if that wasn't enough, the paramilitaries weighed in with their threats. First, it turned out it was an old UDA pub, and then, when I was getting the renovations done, they didn't like it when one of their brethren walked past and heard Irish music coming from the club; the sinners were some workmen from Ardoyne I'd hired. I might as well have desecrated an altar. They posted threats on our new Facebook page. They were going to burn the place to the ground, they said, and I was to be burned at the stake.

Belfast has changed? Yeah, right. And then, which *was* an education, the gay mafia weighed in. Someone piled on to the original threat post saying I was going to do gay nights at the club, which was the cue for some homophobes to let rip. Well, they weren't banking on me being a school friend of Tony 'Dockyard Delores' Wilson. Once he came in on the post, as Dockyard Delores, the gay mafia, I call them them Pink Panthers, went to work, then all the Protestant and Catholic mas with gay kids formed a frontline of attack, and it was conversation over.

No-one takes on a Belfast ma. There's a power shift in

Northern Ireland alright, but maybe not the one everyone keeps banging on about.

'Did you see the weird psychic guy?' I ask Rachel. 'Or was he on after you left?'

I look at Rachel; she's lost in thought. I'm tired of thinking and want to talk.

'Well, when he first came backstage, he pulled me to the side and said the water under Cliftonville Circus told him a message for me from my parents, that soon that same water would be carrying me away. I thanked him and sent *him* on his merry way. Clearly barking, right? Just like your husband.'

No answer. Too soon?

I think my problem is I listen to other people. And I'm too nice. Then people take advantage; it's human nature, I get it, but at some point I'll have to wise up, as my old ma used to say. My first mistake, though, was buying our old house. Sentimental old fool. Which is linked to the being nice, isn't it? Coming home made me think of my ma, and my da, though he and I were never as close. Sean says I did it out of some sort of guilt for abandoning the family, but not all of us are like him. You fly from the nest for a reason. I've never heard of birds building a nest a couple of trees away from the nest they were pushed out of. You fly away. That's the point. And he never got it, poor sod. I feel sorry for him. Even that one time I saw he actually went on holiday and left Ireland, the photos online were of him with other pasty white guys going pinker every day outside Irish pubs eating burgers and chips.

If only I'd done my research on the pub. If only I'd gone for that thorough survey on the house, instead of the quick buy, I'd have found out that under that fresh paint in that old house, damp was spreading up and down the walls from the ground and the roof. That's my life. A litany of 'if onlys'.

'So, go on, give me the gory details,' Rachel says.

'Are you sure? It's pretty out-there,' I tell her, and she nods, and looks back out her window.

Rachel had slipped offstage during Frank's disappearing act, got into the back of my car and hidden herself under some coats, where she waited for me to come when the coast was clear.

'Well, when you weren't where you were supposed to be, your Frank was left scratching his head, and his magic act was over. Dockyard Delores rushed on, and while she told a few jokes and introduced the next act, Frank was ushered off and planted on a chair with a pint. He was staring off into space, repeating 'She's in the magic circle' over and over again. Completely barko!'

No reaction from Rachel. The atmosphere in the car is off.

'The gymnast didn't show as she decided to go back to the Czech Republic before the show even started, there was a comedian who died a death and got booed off, an impressionist who only did Sean Connery for a whole ten minutes, the singer was brilliant and everyone thought she was a shoe-in, but then you'll never guess who ended up winning,' I say. 'The Irish dancer!'

Still, nothing.

'It was pretty incredible. It was this dance called The Kilkenny Races. She was dancing around the stage to this diddly-dee music and, I don't know, she began to do these movements with her legs, pawing her feet on the floor like a horse, and then she, well, began to canter and prance, and then she took a jump over a fence, and she went to take another, but got scared and backed off and, I know it's hard to believe, but everyone was behind this horse to make it, like it really mattered to us all. And when she finally made it, the place went wild. You'd have thought they were watching Ireland win the World Cup.'

I realise I must sound like I've lost it now.

'And the judge, Old Mrs Reid, hard as nails, usually, as you know, was moved to tears. She got up and gave a speech about being bribed, but she wouldn't go through with it because the dance was so powerful the young girl had to win. Saoirse, I think the dancer's name was, then got up and made a speech about that Greta whatshername, and then said she wanted to share the prize money with all the contestants. That's when I ran for the car.' I leave out the bit about me being the one who offered the bribe. I was then going to expose it and refuse to give out the prize money!

I'm just thinking: I can't go back there after I drop her at the ferry. I can't face them all. They can sell off the club and the house to pay who's owed. Sean can handle it and keep any leftovers.

The dark flat water of the lough appears on the left.

Hold on, what did the medium say? Water would be taking me away? Scotland could be where I'll finally find the luck, I know has been waiting for me. Hiding from me all of my life.

This time could be different. I've seen the way Rachel looks at me. I'd be doing it with someone this time. We could be a modern-day Bonnie and Clyde. Me and her against the world.

There's that familiar buzz. That thrill. I'm invincible. The world is my oyster. Ours. Our oyster.

I pull into the car queue for the ferry, and we are still with the engine running. She looks over her shoulder, her face hidden from me. I take her hand and as she turns back to me, I don't wait to see her reaction. I feels her eyes on me as I look straight ahead.

Acknowledgements

I'M VERY GRATEFUL to the Arts Council of Northern Ireland who funded me whilst writing some of the stories in this collection and have supported me over the years to develop my writing. Thank you also to the Arts Council of Ireland who funded me whilst writing *The Circus*.

Thank you to BBC Radio Ulster who commissioned all of the stories included in *I Hear You*, especially Heather Larmour and Michael Shannon.

To Tony Flynn who read three of the stories over the years and whose voice I hear when I write. To the excellent Northern Irish actors who brought the stories alive – in story order; Liam McMahon, Ruby Campbell, Abigail McGibbon, Leeanne Devlin, Chris Robinson, Maggie Cronin, Michael Condron, Michael Patrick, Louise Parker and Ian Beattie.

To Chris, Jen and Kirsty Hamilton-Emery at Salt publishing for all your hard work on this collection.

Thanks to Cavehill Writing Services for their work on the text.

To Cathy Galvin and Word Factory for my love of the short story and for the huge support in writing them. To No Alibis bookshop for getting behind *The Good Son* paving the way for this collection.

Thanks to Anna Burtt and Laura Lockington for advice and generosity.

To Lucy Caldwell, Kit de Waal, Venessa Gebbie, Jackie Kay, Bernie McGill and Alison Moore who have all said nice things about my stories on paper or in person, it really does make a difference.

Thank you to my family for all their support while writing these and all the years that got me here.

Tickles was commissioned by Heather Larmour for BBC Radio 4 and subsequently published by *The London Magazine.*

Cuckoo was commissioned by Michael Shannon for BCC Radio 4 and subsequently published in the *Same Same But Different* anthology.

Daddy Christmas was commissioned by BBC Radio 4 and was subsequently published in *The Irish Times* December 2024.

The Circus was commissioned by Michael Shannon for BBC Radio 4 and this is its first publication.

This book has been typeset by
SALT PUBLISHING LIMITED
using Granjon, a font designed by George W. Jones
for the British branch of the Linotype
company in the United Kingdom. It has been
manufactured using Holmen Book Cream
65gsm paper, and printed and bound by Clays
Limited in Bungay, Suffolk, Great Britain.

CROMER
GREAT BRITAIN
MMXXV